IN THE HOLE

BEN LEVIN

Jumpmaster Press
Birmingham, AL

Library Cataloging Data
Names: Levin, Ben (Ben Levin) 2002 -
Title: In the Hole/ Ben levin
5.5 in. × 8.5 in. (13.97 cm × 21.59 cm)
Description: Jumpmaster Press™ digital eBook edition | Jumpmaster Press™ Trade paperback edition | Alabama: Jumpmaster Press™, 2018.
P.O Box 1774 Alabaster, AL 35007 info@jumpmasterpress.com
Summary: Life goes from great to *worst* for nine-year-old David Kimball when his father loses the family restaurant and consequently their home. Over time and through the support of their community, family, and hard work, David develops the internal strength and outward skills needed to help his family triumph over dire circumstances.
ISBN-13: 978-1-949184-55-6 (eBook) | 978-1-949184-50-1 (paperback) |
1. YA Fiction 2. Economic Recovery 3. Motivational 4. Pandemic Fiction 5. Self-Help 6. Teenage Author 7. Breakout Novel

Printed in the United States of America

For more information on Ben Levin
www.benlevinauthor.com @benlevinauthor

IN THE
HOLE

BEN LEVIN

For all the kids out there *without* homes,
to let you know there is hope.

Contents

1. Loss
2. Evicted
3. Robbed!
4. The Truth Comes Out
5. David Kimball, Businessman
6. Fashion Mishaps
7. A New School
8. Bully Problems
9. Julia in Trouble
10. Slow Spring Recovery
11. Camp Poverty Escape
12. Chef Kimball, Jr.
13. The Restaurant
14. Rising
Epilogue
Acknowledgments
*Resources for Unsheltered People and Families, and
for Good Souls Who Want to
Learn More About the Homelessness Crisis*
Questions for Book Club Study

1

Loss

It was autumn 2009. I was eight years old and about to hear some devastating news.

"Yee-haw!" yelled five-year-old Julia, goofing around and skipping all over the living room like a crazy person. As usual, my sister was being annoying—a total pain in the neck. I wanted to show her my feelings and really let her know that she was bugging me. I assessed my options: (a) whack Julia with my baseball bat to get her to stop, or (b) leave the room and go play video games in my room with headphones to drown out the racket she was making. Or maybe even (c) go over to my best friend Justin O'Malley's house.

Of course, I knew what the best option was. I left the room and picked up the phone.

"Hello? Justin?"

"What's up, David?" Justin asked.

"You want to go to the park?" I asked.

"Sure!" Justin replied. "Baseball?"

I was definitely all over that idea, yet I didn't want to play only baseball.

"Let's shoot hoops too, okay?"

"Sure, I'll bring my basketball," said Justin. "See you in a few."

I already had my orange baseball bat in my hands, so I went and found my baseball and my year-old glove—it all fit in my backpack. I rode off to the park to meet up with Justin. On arrival, Justin was easy to spot, due to his orange sweatpants. His Cubs cap kept falling off his head as he tossed a ball up and down.

"Hey, man, where's your bat?" I called out from the bench. Justin's face fell.

"I left it at practice yesterday," he explained. "I'm sorry, Dave."

"It's okay, Justin," I reassured him. "We can use mine."

At top speed, we raced to the baseball diamond. Although it was October, the weather was clear and balmy—perfect for baseball. Justin commanded the pitcher's mound like a pro and practiced throwing his ball into the air and catching it as I ambled over to home plate. Since I had brought the bat, we agreed it was fair that I get to go first. Justin pitched, and the ball skimmed the bat and rolled foul.

"Foul ball," Justin called. Then he threw it again and I missed completely. "Strike two!" he bellowed.

I know, Justin, you don't have to rub it in, I thought. The next time, I hit the ball and it bounced off third base and past a tree and into the woods. By the time Justin got it, I'd reached home plate.

"David, that was killer! Impressive!" Justin praised.

"Thanks, Justin," I responded, a big smile across my face.

After that I had a few strikes and fouls, before managing to make it to first base. By the time I struck out, the score was two to zero. I ran over to the pitcher's mound. I pitched and Justin swung and hit the ball, placing it slightly past second base. On that round, Justin almost made it home before I tagged him out.

"Whoa," he said panting. "You're fast, man!"

"Thanks," I said proudly.

The sun faded, and the wind swept up. In fact, it was strong enough that as I walked onto home plate, my baseball cap flew up into the air, higher than I would have expected.

"My hat!" I gasped. I ran as fast as I could. After a minute, my hat floated downward. It landed on what looked like Canadian goose poop. I picked up my cap by its top. Thankfully, it didn't stink, even though the green poop stains looked absolutely disgusting! There was no way I could wear it anymore!

"All set, dude?" Justin asked as I reached the diamond.

"Yeah. It landed in bird crap. It's ruined!" I complained, adding, "I'm going home to get a new hat. I'll call you, okay?"

"Aw, c'mon Dave," Justin groaned. "Hoops first, okay?"

I'd forgotten about basketball and nodded. "Okay."

After I completely destroyed Justin in three rounds of *Horse*, we decided to call it a day and I biked home.

When I got home, I immediately went to find Mom. I found her in the living room working on a painting. My mom loves to paint. Usually, she paints pictures of our family or Bible scenes—Mom is religious and very devoted to her faith. She also paints things according to her mood or related to holidays, such as turkey images for Thanksgiving and fireworks for Fourth of July. She had often expressed a desire to be a professional painter, still she's too self-conscious about her artwork.

"Hey, Mom," I called.

"Hey, honey, are you okay?" she asked, noticing the look on my face.

I told her what had happened. "No way can I wear this anymore," I announced. "Can I please get a new one?"

"I'm sorry, sweetie, I don't think we have the money," my mother replied, turning abruptly back to her painting.

"For a cap?!" I felt really upset. I hardly ever asked for anything, yet this was the third time in a row that my parents had said no to me. Just one week before, when Mom took Julia and me to the grocery store, and we'd both asked for cookies, Mom had said no. Then, the week after school started, I'd asked Dad if he could take me, and maybe Justin too, to a nearby baseball game (Tigers vs. Reds), and he had said no. He told us that it was because he had to work. (In the end, Mr. O'Malley, Justin's dad, had taken us.)

Now, on strike three, I lost my temper.

"Mom, why do you guys always say no? I never even ask for that much!" I burst out. "It's not fair!"

Mom turned back to me, a sad look in her eyes. "Honey, there's something we've been trying to figure out how to tell you and your sister," she said softly.

I paused nervously wondering what was coming next, as Mom took a deep breath.

"What is it, Mom?"

"David," she said, "you need to know that Dad lost his job."

"What?" I was confused. "How could Dad get fired? He *owns* the place!" My dad owned a popular diner in our neighborhood.

Mom took a deep breath. "David, do you remember Mr. Hawthorne? The man who used to work for our diner?"

"The nutty guy who was always cracking jokes about how he would kill someone?" I asked.

Mom nodded. "The truth is, David—do you know what drugs are?"

"A little. Well, not really, Mom. What are they?"

"Sometimes reckless or irresponsible people take certain pills or drinks, or even foods, and they sometimes become irrational. Mr. Hawthorne was one of them. Maybe you recall his antics—?"

"I remember he often acted bizarre and even hollered at that little girl when she dropped her food."

Mom nodded and took a deep, slow breath before she spoke again. "David..." she said cautiously, "...that girl is the girl who went missing a while back. Do you remember it was in the news?" I nodded, confused. My mom caught herself as she choked on a sob. "When people in Wood Creek learned that Mr. Hawthorne was abusing drugs, they concluded that the girl's disappearance was *his* doing. The diner got a bad reputation because of what happened. People stopped trusting your father to hire responsible people, and we lost a ton of business. David, the diner closed around the end of August."

"Whoaaa," is all I could utter. I'd been too involved in back-to-school stuff to notice the shift. And right now, I was too stunned to speak.

Mom hugged me for a long time before she continued, "Recently, your father sold his antique chess set, camera, and his golf clubs along with a few other things, to earn enough money to pay the rent. I am sorry, honey..." Mom looked sad. "We definitely can't afford luxuries like baseball caps right now. But I can wash it for you."

"Okay, Mom," I said. "Thanks for telling me." Mom just kept hugging me. "Mom," I ventured to ask, "What should I do now for my friends' birthday presents?"

"Maybe you could make them something?" Mom offered.

"Okay," I replied, crestfallen, and murmured, "Thanks for the idea." Deep inside, I felt like crying. I was officially poor—boy, did that news sting!

As I left the kitchen, Mom called out, "Just remember one thing, honey. No matter what, our family is sticking together. Your father and I will always be here for you and your sister."

"Thanks, Mom," I mumbled. I guess I was still in shock and feeling pretty powerless.

When I got to school on Tuesday morning, my friends were all circled around a contraption, and looking pretty riveted. All eyes on one focus is a sure sign that something downright spellbinding is going on!

I spotted Justin in the group and stood by him.

"What's going on?" I whispered.

"Otto just got a really cool toy, a remote-control airplane!"

At that moment, stocky brown-haired Otto Gutierrez spotted me. "Oh, good. David's here. Now we can launch."

Otto placed a beautiful blue toy airplane on the ground.

I gasped. The airplane was magnificent—one of the most awesome toys I had ever seen. It was bigger than most toy airplanes. It even had a miniature person inside of it!

"Everyone, count to three!" Otto called out.

"One! Two! Three!" we chanted.

Otto activated his remote control and the plane zoomed upward, flying high, low, up, down, left, right. Otto was a capable pilot. I was impressed.

"Otto, where'd you get it?" asked Max Clemente. "I want to buy one."

"ToysRUs," Otto replied. "Maybe we could all go together this weekend and buy some and have an aerial race!"

"Yeah, all of us will buy one!"

"Let the games begin!"

Everyone jumped in, talking over each other, planning aerial championships! The guys jabbered endlessly about "how cool it's gonna be when we all have one." I felt left out since I could not afford one. It's hard not to resent your friends when they can afford toys that you are too poor to buy.

I made a quick decision.

"Oh, hey guys, I've gotta hit the boy's room. See you in class!" I bolted into school through the back door.

Justin ran to catch up.

"David, are you okay?" I sighed.

"Justin, wanna know why your dad and not mine took us to the game the other day?"

"Why?" Justin asked. I was embarrassed; still, I had to tell him the truth.

"My dad lost his job six weeks ago. And I only heard last weekend."

"Whoa," said Justin. "I'm really sorry, dude."

"Thanks," I said. "Please don't tell anyone."

"Can I tell Robby?" Justin asked. I thought about that. I didn't want Justin telling the news to too many people. After some thought, I realized I had to let Justin tell Robby. Robby was Justin's other best friend. Plus, they are cousins and Justin felt that he couldn't keep a secret from a relative. Besides, I was friends with Robby too, and I knew he wasn't a gossip.

"Only Robby and your parents," I said firmly. "No one else. Got it?"

"Got it, bro!" Justin affirmed. We shook hands.

Soon thereafter, Julia came home from her friend Rose's house and said, "Mommy, I have a request."

"Hi, hon, what is it?" Mom asked.

"Well, today Rose's mom took us to the toy store. She bought Rose a stuffed deer and me a stuffed kitten. I'm really thankful that Rose bought this kitty cat for me. Can we buy her something in return, like a doll?"

"Julia, honey," Mom replied, sounding kind of irritated, "you do not have to buy someone something in return the moment they give you a gift." She looked sad again. "Can you make Rose a doll, sweetheart?"

"That's not the same!" Julia cried.

"You'd be making something special with your own hands," Mom added gently.

"It still doesn't feel like enough!" Julia pouted, sticking out her lower lip.

"I'm sorry. The truth is, Julia, we just don't have the money."

Julia looked even sadder than Mom, and asked, "Why, Mommy? Why don't we have the money!?" I knew my little sister was about to be told the terrible truth, so I decided to leave the room. I felt sorry for Julia. She couldn't repay her friend for the generous present. Of course, Julia would write a thank-you note for the gift. Even so, I knew it wasn't the same as spending money on someone.

Things felt completely off key. We couldn't even keep luxuries we already owned. Within the first few minutes after entering my bedroom that night, I noticed something was missing. Until that moment, my room had always been my personal sanctuary that completely represented me. At that time, I had four main hobbies: video games, baseball, basketball, and writing. I had notebooks all over my bed, and usually wrote a little each night before going to bed. In one corner of my room, I had arranged my baseball equipment with care. I taped photos of Babe Ruth, Barry Bonds, and other sports heroes of mine along the walls of that corner. My parents let me put a Nerf basketball net on my bedroom door, so I could shoot hoops whenever I wanted.

Sometimes, when Justin or another friend slept over, I set up a second Nerf basketball net on the wall so we could play together. I kept a special basketball next to my bed.

And, I had a PlayStation—or at least I thought I had. That evening, however, I realized my PlayStation was missing. I figured Mom or Dad had hidden it to get me to sleep at night and not go on video games. I decided to ask them about it the next day, and slept restlessly. The next morning, I found Mom in the kitchen making muffins, and I approached her.

"Mom, my PlayStation's missing."

"Oh, David," Mom replied, looking guilty. "I'm sorry I didn't ask you yet. Your father had to take some of Julia's and your belongings to help us get money. But don't worry, I came up with a compromise. We stowed your stuff to sell, and we won't sell it until you give us permission."

Dad walked in and added brightly, "And possession is 90% of ownership!" Then, looking very seriously into my eyes, he asked, "Dav-o, is this okay?"

I thought about it. I loved video games and couldn't imagine life without them. Deep in my heart, however, I knew it was the right thing to do to help my family. Besides, I could always play at a friend's house if I wanted.

Choking back tears, I conceded, "Sure, Dad."

I have a theory that every boy in the 21st century cries when he loses or breaks his Xbox or PlayStation. What I know for a fact is that when I asked if I could say goodbye to my PlayStation and Dad said yes, I burst into tears the minute I started hugging it. I hoped someone else would enjoy it every bit as much as I had, so I wouldn't have made that painful sacrifice for nothing. Mom told me if I was that obsessed with a machine, I probably needed to get a life, even though I'd grown up with video games and I loved them. They were a huge part of my life, and I thought that after having known me for eight years, my need for video games would have been crystal clear to her!

Soon thereafter, at Dad's yard sale, I found some of my other belongings—like my old football, the stuffed baboon I slept with when I was four, and the ice cream maker my family had bought when vacationing in Virginia two summers ago. I also saw some of Julia's old Barbie dolls and princess costumes on the table at the yard sale.

Monday morning at school, it seemed that the seating chart had been changed. I normally would have been a little frustrated with the fact that Stacey, whom I found annoying, was my seat-mate. This morning, however, I was too bummed about losing my PlayStation to think about anything else. Being hard up financially was really taking a bite out of my life. What got me out of my funk was a need to care for Mom.

Since I couldn't even afford to buy school lunches anymore, Mom began staying up late to make bag lunch for Julia and me. She couldn't make them during the day because she was busy looking for extra work to help pay the bills. That was bad news for me, because lack of sleep was making my mother cranky.

The following Wednesday I slept in late, because I was having a wonderful dream about playing for the Bulls. Abruptly, though, my slumber was disrupted when Mom pulled off my sheet.

"Wake up!" she hollered roughly. "You can't be late for school!"

I was alarmed. Mom had never yelled at me before.

"Mom, please don't shout. It's scary," I began.

"You think the mother who gave birth to you is scary?" yelled Mom.

"Just when you shout," I replied nervously. "I'm not used to it."

"Well, grow up!" Mom snapped.

As upsetting as it was, I tried listening to Mom until I went to school, which wasn't easy because she kept screaming and that was freaking me out.

The truth was, Mom needed me. She was also worried because Halloween was right around the corner and she was feeling pressured about needing to buy candy for the Trick-or-Treaters. She and Dad were baking their special plum cupcakes instead, with a recipe that had been passed down in my dad's family. It was a little unusual to give homemade goods on Halloween, so Mom was feeling insecure. One evening just before Halloween, she called me in to ask my opinion.

"Is it, um, weird on Halloween to give out cupcakes I baked?" she asked me. I thought about that.

"It's a little different," I replied, trying to be honest. "Mom, everyone loves cupcakes no matter where they're made. I think you'll be fine with cupcakes."

"Really? Are cupcakes acceptable for Halloween, though? Do any of your friends' parents give out homemade food?" Mom pressed.

"Well, no, but I still think it's okay, Mom," I tried to reassure her. "Think of it this way. At least you're not giving out celery and carrots."

Another Halloween issue was, what was I going to wear? I couldn't go as myself and let everyone guess that I didn't have enough money for a Halloween costume. I wrote down a list of possible ideas: Andre Iguodala (at that time, a member of the 76ers, an NBA team who wore red uniforms. My uniform for my basketball league was red and we both had a Number 4 jersey). Another option was a homemade ghost costume, or my costume from last year, a dog. After I ran this by Mom, she had an amazing idea. She could make me a paper elephant trunk and ears and I could wear all greyish blue, and be an elephant for Halloween! I thought it was a terrific idea and my anxiety subsided.

As a five-year-old, Julia didn't have my issue because every single year, she had the same costume: a horse. I do not know anyone as horse-crazy as my sister. Her favorite toys were a rocking horse and a stuffed horse. Her walls were plastered with horse posters and her shelves were full of horse books. With the exception of Sundays, Julia took riding lessons every single day. There was a woman named Caroline who lived nearby and owned a stable where she gave free riding lessons to elementary school girls in exchange for the girls feeding and grooming the horses and mucking the stalls.

Justin suggested we have a scary sleepover for Halloween. I agreed.

"Who else will come?" I asked.

"Robby, Max, and the rest of the guys," replied Justin.

"Sounds really cool, Justin!" I smiled. "We should definitely do it!"

In the end, with the exception of Otto who had been forced by his mom to trick-or-treat with his twin sister, all the guys in our class were able to come. In addition, a few of our fourth-grade friends came too. Robby, Justin, and I agreed to meet up with them at Justin's house. For Halloween, Justin was a baseball player and Robby came as President Abraham Lincoln. And I, in my elephant costume, was really excited about Halloween since I had not had candy in ages!

Justin and Robby arrived at my house at five. They rang the doorbell and I answered.

"Hey, David," said Robby, "Nice trunk."

"Thanks," I said. I gave both of their costumes a quick once-over, wondering how easy it would have been to tell them apart had they been wearing the same thing. They were both tall, had short wavy dark hair, and chestnut brown eyes, and almost always wore baseball jerseys. Robby's a little thicker than Justin, and he's tan while Justin is freckled. After I was done examining their costumes, I said, "Come on, let's go!"

The three of us walked out into the night, thankfully before Mom arrived, so I avoided arguing with her about how much candy I could eat. Within the first twenty minutes, our bags were loaded, and I was already eating my chocolate bars in order to have room in my bag for other candy—at least that was what I told myself. After thirty minutes of plundering, we arrived at Justin's.

Mrs. O'Malley was waiting. "Hi, boys," she said. When Justin and Robby turned their backs, she gave me a twenty-dollar bill. "Justin told me," she whispered, "Give this to your mother, okay?"

"Okay," I said, embarrassed. Secretly, I was grateful for the O'Malley family's kindness toward my family.

The other boys arrived. The fourth graders were all dressed as superheroes. Pale, sandy-haired Sam Erring, for example, was dressed in a dark blue batman suit, and Louis Allen, who was Black and had a straight nose and fairly big arms for a ten-year-old, was dressed as the hero Cyborg, with metal on his face and everything. Eliot

Rogers and Max wore Dracula costumes. Max was really the better Count Dracula, I thought, because he was tall and had straight Presley-ish black hair. Eliot was a good vampire too, though his healthy complexion and curly bangs looked a little out of place on Count Dracula. Nick Lance, a tall skinny blonde guy I'd been friends with since we were three, was dressed up as Lionel Messi, the soccer player.

"Doesn't Messi have a beard, Nick?" I asked. Nick shrugged.

"I don't have any fake beards," he told me, "and Mom wouldn't let me borrow her makeup."

We all sat in the living room and went through our candy. I had countless Smarties, M&Ms, and Almond Joys.

"Hey, Justin, how did your mom agree to let you paint the sofas for Halloween?" Louis asked, staring at the couches. Justin had given all the sofas and chairs a black and orange stripe motif. It was perfect for Halloween. Justin laughed.

"It was actually my mom's idea, Louis. She was feeling very into the Halloween mood this year and she thought it would be a cool way to celebrate the holiday. Also, they're really old and we are getting new furniture anyway." *Lucky*, I thought wistfully. I wished my family could afford new furniture!

"Your mom actually proposed the idea of painting the couches?" Nick asked in amazement. "That's crazy!! My mom would have thrown a fit if Sienna or I had done something like this!"

"Same," I agreed. Next we decided to write out some spooky poems and stories and then share them with each other. Justin grabbed paper and pens from the living room shelves, and we began. I looked outside and saw several ghosts and goblins pass by. There was a little deer in the group, too. As the only deer in the group, the kid looked completely out-of-place with all the monsters, which inspired me to write this:

Out-of-Place!
I'm all alone, in a haunted house, the only beautiful
face,
The only thing not frightening, I am out-of-place,
Little tiny Pluto in outer space,
With these ghosts and vampires, I'm out of place,
Scary little monsters ready to eat me in every phase,
That's why I am completely out-of-place.

I passed my poem to Eliot and I read Nick's story. His was about a monster playing soccer. His word choice was pretty charming and actually kind of ingenious, and totally made me laugh. He had written sentences like, "His feet seemed to growl almost as loud as his mouth as he kicked the ball." Robby's story was also funny. It was about a talking ice cream cone that screamed and terrified every kid who tried to eat him. I'm not completely sure it was spooky, but it definitely made me laugh! After we finished reading each other's pieces, we watched a movie about a ghost who, during his lifetime, had been quite the Bulls player and won several NBA Championships. During the movie, one by one, we fell asleep on the sleeping bags Justin's mom had put out for each of us.

We awoke the next morning to the delicious aroma of sizzling bacon.

"Take as much as you want if the candy hasn't filled you up for the entire month of November!" called Mrs. O'Malley.

"Thanks, Mom," said Justin.

"By the way, David," Mrs. O'Malley added, leaning her head into the room, "Nick's dad, Mr. Lance, will give you a ride home."

"Thanks, Mrs. O'Malley," I said.

After Nick's dad dropped me off, I noticed an odd difference in our driveway. My dad's Jeep was missing. That was strange, because Mom and Dad were both home. Mom came into the living room and cupped my face in her hands.

"You noticed, didn't you?" she asked me, her forehead furrowed with worry. "Honey, we had to sell it."

"Mom," I asked, feeling frantic, "how will we get around?"

"A neighbor is lending us a Honda Fit until we get back on our feet," said Mom. "And with a smaller car, we don't have to pay as much for gas."

I could not believe it. I'd just been inside Nick's family's gigantic automobile that could fit two families of four, and now my family suddenly had a super tiny car that looked like it was some kind of toy? That was hard for me to take in. I was still trying to keep my lack of money a secret from my friends. Now, I could no longer offer rides without divulging my big secret. That hurt. I had shared my situation with Justin, and *only* Justin. I didn't want anyone else to know.

A month later, when we returned to school from Thanksgiving week, my third-grade teacher, Ms. Wallow, asked me to write an essay called *A Christmas Wish*. Well, it didn't take me long to assess what was valuable and important to me. I knew right away and wrote at the top, "*A Job for My Dad or Maybe My Mom.*"

When I showed Ms. Wallow, she said, "That's all?"

I nodded blankly. Even though some stores do have sales around holiday time, it seemed to me at the time that a Christmas List was not meant for someone living in poverty.

2

Evicted

Even though my family and I were now poor, life continued. For Christmas, I got new sneakers from my neighbors. The sneakers had originally been for my neighbor's son, whose parents had wanted him to play basketball. As it turned out, he had no interest and we had the same shoe size, so our neighbors gave the shoes to me instead. Also, on January 5th, I turned nine and to celebrate, my friends and I watched basketball with popcorn drenched in butter.

Plus, not even being poor could take away my happiness about a certain fact: my Owls basketball team's season was finally here. As a basketball player, I may have been short, still, I was really, really fast and extremely coordinated. I also had a great shot. And even though I wasn't getting as much food as I was used to, I was only hungry sometimes and I felt like my skills were increasing by the minute. By January, I'd played four games with my club team, and even started in one of them (most games, I was the first sub).

The week after my birthday, my friends and I had a game against the Northeastern Wood Creek Barbarians. They were our worst enemies in the Community Basketball League and we were determined to beat them!

"David, guess what?" Justin said as we walked to the community center. "Ryan the Giant is sick, so the Owls just might beat the Barbarians today!"

"Yes!" I yelled, punching my fist into the air.

Ryan the Giant was the captain of the Barbarians, and he definitely had the potential to be an NBA star when he grew up. He was already five feet, eight inches tall, and he was only in fourth grade. The last time we played their team, we lost by a landslide, and Ryan the Giant had done the majority of the scoring. In fact, with as much talent as he had, it was impossible to keep from admiring him—even *just* a little.

Upon arrival, we shook hands with Coach Barry before getting right to warm-ups. Two minutes before the game, Coach Barry tapped my shoulder.

"Dave," he said, "Did you know that Pete is in Virginia this week?" (Pete Zimmerman, a fourth grader and good friend, was our starting point guard.)

"Yes, I did know that," I replied, wondering what Coach Barry was getting at.

"That means *you're* starting today!" Coach Barry exclaimed. "You've gotten really good these past few weeks!" He patted my shoulder proudly and I beamed.

"Thank you," I murmured shyly.

Coach Barry continued praising me, "I'm grateful for your dedication and grit. Good luck out there."

Game Time: I stood on the court with my hands on my hips.

The ref yelled, "One! Two! Three!" and threw the ball.

The center on the other team snatched the ball. I noticed on the back of his jersey the number *21* and the last name *Brintain*. (In our league, we were all given a jersey with our last name on it.) Brintain sprinted across the court so quickly that he looked like he was flying. We hadn't even been playing for fifteen seconds before the score was 2 - 0.

As the ball swished through the hoop, Brintain waved at the audience and yelled, "And that's how I, Joseph Brintain, do it!"

I was disgusted. *What a showoff!* I thought.

The ref passed me the ball, and I passed it to Louis who dribbled and scored a three. Shortly after that, Sam Erring scored another three-pointer, bouncing the ball off the backboard, and then we slowly began to dominate.

The quarter was halfway through when Louis passed to me.

Suddenly, the boy I was guarding whispered to me, "Whatcha playing basketball for, *Hobbit*?"

My face turned red. With the sudden desire to show him how wrong he was to belittle me for my size, I took a deep breath, did a little dribbling, threw the ball into the air, and *swish*: the ball plunked into the hoop. Now we were leading 9 - 2.

"Nice shot!" Coach cheered. Then, addressing all of us, he added, "Keep it up, guys! With your skills and hustle, we are on the road to winning!"

By the end of the quarter, we were ahead by ten points. Coach put Nick in for Max and Justin in for Louis, and we started up again.

By the last quarter of the game, we were ahead by more than thirty points. I'd scored a few of them, including a foul shot. In fact, by the last quarter, all of the players on our team had gotten at least a minute of playing time. It was not long before the starters were back on the court. I made my last shot with two minutes left, and the game ended with the score 55 - 33, Owls. We were thrilled! In fact, our euphoria over the win lasted almost a week. Well, my teammates' happiness lasted. Mine lasted until that night—when my mom picked me up looking sad.

"Mom? What's wrong?" I asked, my grin fading as we walked away from school toward the car. Mom took a deep breath.

"I have been struggling to figure out how to tell you this all afternoon. I wanted to wait until after the game to tell you the news. Come on." I instantly forgot about the game. I knew something was really wrong. I just knew.

Julia and Dad were in the car. Dad looked miserable, and Julia looked very confused. We drove to our house. When we got to my driveway, it was blocked by a large open truck. Inside were our couches, beds, tables, chairs, and toys. A few things, like the kiddie bookshelf with the stars on it, still stood on the driveway. Most of our stuff was inside the truck. I jumped out of the car and peered inside the house. All the furniture was gone.

That was when I realized the truth: we had been evicted. Thrown out. I felt humiliated as it sank in. It hurt like crazy! I was stunned!

How could this have happened? I wondered.

After a long silence, I asked, "Were we even warned?"

"We were warned. But we didn't tell you because we hoped we'd get the money for the late mortgage payments in time," Mom replied softly, "Last night, your father and I realized that we simply can't make those payments right now. So, this morning, while you were in school, we, along with a few friends, packed all our things. We're going to store most of this stuff with our relatives."

Julia then asked, "Can we stay in our house anyway? Without our furniture?" She then announced firmly, "I'm going in right now!" Julia was too young to understand we simply weren't allowed inside anymore.

"Julia, no," Mom said quietly, "We're not allowed to stay here anymore. But it's okay, because we're all together, and we'll find a new home."

Tears ran down my cheeks. *We were homeless!* To me, being homeless was the worst thing that could ever happen to someone. I was also afraid of how it might affect my grades. How could I possibly do my homework if we didn't have a *home*?

Where can we go? Are we nomads now? Thousands of questions flooded my brain.

"Are we going to... live in the car?" I asked.

"For now, we will have to," replied Mom softly. "Unless or until we find a shelter or a generous friend with enough space to house all four of us for a while."

To my surprise, Dad drove the car to our local church. Nobody spoke. The silence was worse than anything.

"Um, Dad?" I asked as Dad shut off the engine in the parking lot. "What are we doing here on a school day?"

"For the time being, the church is going to be our new base," he said. "Your mom spoke to the pastor, and he has agreed to allow us to stay here for as long as we need. So here's the plan. We'll sleep in the car at night and use it to drive to and from school. We'll use the church's bathrooms for sponge baths and to change clothes, and we'll do homework in the social hall."

"Isn't that prohibited?" I asked nervously.

It could not have been more horrible and humiliating!

"The church is supporting us, at least for right now. So it's okay," replied Dad.

"And, right this moment," Mom added, "we have no other option."

Julia frowned, trying to take in what our parents were saying. Then her young mind shifted to her belly. "What about dinner?"

"We'll have to ask permission to bring our own food in, and if they agree, we'll eat after homework. Otherwise, we will eat in the car," Mom informed us.

I shuddered.

As much as I love Dad, I did not look forward to sleeping in a car, within earshot of his snores. Once, when I was five, we had visitors take my room for a week, so I slept with my parents. And let me tell you, Dad wheezed so loudly that it's a miracle Mom was always cheerful in the morning. Not to mention the fact that changing into my PJs in a public place felt traumatic. I wondered if it would be preferable to wear the same clothes all the time. Was this really my new life? I hoped like crazy it would be temporary.

I felt absolutely devastated. Even when things were tight, Mom and Dad always put Julia's and my well-being first. Even that horrid first night, for dinner Mom and Dad shared a tuna sandwich plus some carrots and celery, and they gave Julia and me peanut butter and jelly sandwiches.

Forever a picky eater, Julia wrinkled her nose and asked, "Jelly? Gross! I say *no* to such a yucky dinner, and Aris does, as well!" Aris, her stuffed pony toy, snubbed his nose, too.

"I'm so sorry, honey, that's all we have," Mom replied.

Never one to go down without a fight, my little sister continued to argue for the next twenty minutes about having *such a yucky dinner.*

Finally, Dad stepped in and said, "It's okay, Charlotte, I'll go buy Julia a *Happy Meal.*"

Mom protested, "Harry, we can't afford—" Dad shot her an anxious look and she clammed, "Fine. Go."

Julia cheered, "Yay! Aris, we're getting a *Happy Meal!*"

At 8:00 p.m. that night, we slunk into the church bathroom to brush our teeth and put on our pajamas. I was relieved no one else was in the bathroom. Then, when I walked to the car in my PJs, I felt like anyone who happened to be at the church might somehow be staring at me. It was a nightmare. I'll never forget that indescribably terrible feeling I had that first night as a homeless person. Not to mention, I could barely sleep in a parking lot with my brain full of doubts and fears—and Dad snoring at eighty decibels!

The worst part was not how bad my family's new conditions were. Without a doubt, the worst part was how living in the car affected me at school. In the third grade at school, we started every day working on a challenge with our seat partner. That month, my partner was Alexa Brewer, a chestnut-brown haired girl who enjoyed fancy clothes, getting good grades... and bullying me. Today our challenge was, "Where does the President live? And what is his address?"

"The White House," I said weakly. I was hungry and tired. Although my mom was trying her best to get us good meals with enough nutrition to carry us through the day, we just didn't have the money to buy the necessary protein, fresh fruits, and vegetables that kids need to function at their best. We were eating a lot of noodles, snack foods, and peanut butter and jelly sandwiches, and it just wasn't carrying me, a growing athlete.

"Right," said Alexa. "What's the address of the White House?"

"What?" I asked.

"What's the address of the White House?"

"I dunno." I shrugged.

Alexa rolled her eyes and chided me, "Come on, David! If you don't try harder, then we'll both get a bad grade! Wake up and try!"

I sighed wearily. I felt exhausted and did not feel like being reprimanded, particularly by the same girl who had been trying to make my life miserable since kindergarten. My fatigue, meanwhile, was growing stronger and causing me to yawn. My head felt as heavy as a thirty-pound weight as I tried to keep myself from resting it on my desk.

Alexa had had enough and slapped her desk angrily. Ms. Wallow walked over.

"Alexa, calm yourself," she said, "Banging your hand against your desk is not permitted in class. Is everything all right?"

"David is being lazy!" Alexa pouted.

"Come now," our teacher replied, "I'm sure he's just having a hard time today. We all struggle to do our best work sometimes." Ms. Wallow then spoke softly to me. "David, you look sleepy. Maybe go splash some water on your face." (By this time, even though I wasn't aware of it, my parents had informed Ms. Wallow about our situation.)

"Yes, ma'am," I said politely, and found my way to the bathroom.

Four days later, in gym class, we were playing kickball. I was defending third base when Eliot was up. Eliot was not a great kickball player. In fact, he was pretty bad, so I was not concerned. However, after Eliot booted the ball, I learned to never underestimate anyone again. The ball flew in my direction, and I caught it. Robby, who was already on first base, was advancing to second.

"Morgan! Catch!" I yelled to Morgan Wilkins who was guarding second base. Morgan tried to catch it. Then, two terrible things happened at once. I was so tired and hungry that my aim was totally off I threw the ball into center field. At the same time, my stomach gurgled *loudly*, which distracted Morgan. Robby and Eliot both made it home, and it was all my fault. I felt super frustrated—at myself, my stupid empty stomach, and at my family's situation!

I was still beating myself up after the game when Justin ran to catch up with me.

"David, has your family gotten so poor that you can't even afford enough to eat?"

"It's worse than that," I sighed. "We lost our home."

"How's that possible?" Justin looked alarmed and concerned. "Where are you sleeping? On the street?"

I told him all about living in a parking lot and using the church for amenities.

Justin was stunned. "I'm so sorry, buddy," he said simply.

The next day, Justin brought me seven baked potatoes.

"Here, these might help make it easier to function," he offered. "Baked'em myself."

"Thanks, Justin." I smiled, relieved that I had told him what had happened, and devoured two of the potatoes immediately. They tasted amazing. Justin had even remembered to add butter and salt!

My only escapes from this difficult life were sports and my friends. I began to appreciate the camaraderie we had and how much my friendships, especially in sports, mattered to me, and I appreciated when friends invited me to hang out. Sitting at Justin's kitchen table and playing *Monopoly* with him felt like a luxury, especially with his mom's veritable conveyor belt of snacks. And I remembered to say *thank you* when Eliot invited me over. I no longer took for granted Nick's invitation for a sleepover, and I looked forward to a warm shower and the soft bed he offered. When I went to my friend Will Yang's house (Will was a year older), I was a lot more grateful, because I felt incredibly relieved to be in a familiar home.

And when I went to the movies with Max and Mr. and Mrs. Clemente, they would buy us hot dogs and corn chips with melted cheese. I was grateful the Clementes let me come along.

I realized that the Clementes and some of my friends' parents knew about our situation and were simply kind enough to not share our personal life with their own children. It is tough to keep secrets in a community as tight as the South Western part of Wood Creek. I had refused to tell Max or any of my friends other than Justin about my situation. As I got increasingly skinny, I think they must have suspected something, though.

Sports and after-school activities also helped my soul a lot. Having gone without adequate food and sleep, my basketball season should have been ruined. Two things, however, prevented that. First, Coach Barry brought snacks. I usually grabbed a couple at every practice and game; I wanted to make sure I would have enough energy to play well. Secondly, the night before each game day, I went to a friend's house to sleepover, preventing my sleep from being ruined by being jammed in the back seat of that tiny car. Plus, I'd get a real solid meal.

The night before my last game, I bunked at Justin's house. Justin's big brother, Eric, was there, and he and Mr. O'Malley were both giving us a pep talk for the last game.

"If you get in the game, make sure to *own* it! And always give *more* than your best effort!" ordered Mr. O'Malley. "Otherwise, you could end up spending way too much time feeling guilty about your mistakes, just like I did when I was your age."

"You better win, Justin, or you're disinherited!" Eric added, jokingly.

"Eric, that's enough! Be nice to your brother," Justin's mom scolded as she looked up from the book she was reading.

"We better go to sleep," I said. "Getting a good night's sleep is an important part of winning."

"Agreed, man," said Justin.

Justin and I sprinted to Justin's room and got ready for bed.

Crawling into his bed, Justin said, "Assuming I can sleep when having your best friend over for a sleepover is as fun as it is."

"I'll go sleep in another room," I offered, climbing into my David Wright sleeping bag. Getting to sleep in *any* room felt like a luxury, given my *new normal*.

"Naw, you can stay here. I was just kidding. Good night, David."

That was when I realized I was missing something.

"Justin," I asked, "could you pass me a pillow?"

"Too tired," mumbled Justin, dozing.

Well! I thought, *Tired doesn't mean you can be rude!* We were best friends after all! I knew exactly how to convince him to help me out since he had confessed to me earlier that he'd done something *devious* the previous week.

I said, mischievously, "Give me a pillow, Justin, or... I'll tell Ms. Wallow that the only reason you got an A+ on the musical instrument quiz was because Danielle showed you her answers!"

Justin sighed. "Fine, David. Pillow *incoming!*" And he smashed one over at me like in volleyball. Laughing, I rolled over and fell quickly into a sound asleep.

The next morning, after driving us to school, Mrs. O'Malley slipped me fifty dollars.

"Give this to your mom," she said. "I'll help out your family whenever I'm able. Every month, I'll send Justin to school with a fifty-dollar bill for your family."

Considering the fact that I lived in a tiny car, which, because we'd been living in it for a month, was starting to smell a little from sweat and food that had gone bad, I did not take this gift for granted.

"Thank you, Mrs. O'Malley," I whispered, "I appreciate it. I know my mom will too."

That school day seemed to go on forever. In fact, I was so impatient in last period (Science) that I begged the teacher to dismiss me and the other boys early for our game. All I could think about was that it was our last basketball game. We'd done pretty well that season, winning slightly more than half our games. Nevertheless, we were determined to beat the Magicians team and win our final game.

When we were dismissed, as fast as we could, my friends and I ran to the community center where our team was assigned to play that day. As soon as we arrived, we got right to work. There was no risk of any of us being sluggish at our last game. I practiced shooting, taking mental note of how often I made it or missed. That way, I could challenge myself.

As Coach gave us one of his sagacious pep talks, his words of wisdom inspiring us, I spotted my parents in the bleachers. *Win this for your parents, David*, I told myself. *Give them the happiness they haven't had in a while.*

The game began with the usual starters: Max, Robby, Pete, Louis, and Sam. Max controlled the ball from the tip-off and then passed to Robby. Robby started dribbling toward a corner. From there, he passed to Sam who was near the basket. Sam then made a dunk and scored 2 - 0. Many excited fans cheered, and when my dad did too, I was the happiest boy alive.

"Yes!" I heard Dad yell. That made my day.

A minute later, Louis scored a basket. 4 - 0. A few seconds later, Coach Barry patted my back.

"David," he whispered. "You're in for Louis."

Nick was also subbing in for Robby. We waited a few seconds, and then after Lucas scored a three-pointer, I went in. Peter passed to me and I passed to Sam. Sam tried to shoot a three. He missed. I got ready to defend. As the boy I was guarding came up, he began trash-talking me.

"Hey, shrimp, I'm six inches taller than you," he jeered. "Which means I'm a lot more aggressive, because all dwarfs are dorks." I realized *he* was completely distracted by his own attempts to intimidate me and so I decided to seize the opportunity! I was fast, faster than he was for sure, and gleefully, I snatched the ball from him before he knew what had happened.

"David! Pass!" yelled Peter.

I passed it to him at once. Peter passed to Sam, who, unfortunately, missed again. The boy who had tried to intimidate me before was dribbling the ball down the court. I was getting ready to defend him when the most awful thing happened: my stomach made a loud growling noise as the boy dribbled past me. Immediately, the thought flashed through my mind: *Oh no! They're going to think I'm starving because I'm homeless!* Looking back now, I realize that (a) nobody probably even heard my stomach growl, and (b) even if they did, there could have been a lot of reasons why my stomach might be growling other than homelessness! At the time, I was, understandably, paranoid.

The boy I was guarding tried to pass the ball to the boy Nick was guarding. Quick as lightning, Nick intercepted the pass, drove the ball to the basket, and scored, so no one seemed to care about my grumbling stomach. My confidence had lapsed. I felt stupefied and humiliated. Why couldn't I concentrate on the ball? I bashed myself for my poor defense and I believed that everyone else did too.

A minute later, Coach Barry called a time out. "David, are you okay?" I nodded.

"Embarrassed that I messed up, I guess."

"David, stop belittling yourself. The only one being hard on you is *you*. We all mess up once in a while. The important thing is we pick ourselves back up and we don't fall behind. Have a second go! You deserve it!" he encouraged.

"No, I don't! I'm mad at myself and I'm pretty sure everyone else is, too!" I replied.

"David, I know you can do it. Now get in there, show everyone that you're a basketball prodigy. Prove me right!" Coach ordered. I was amazed he believed in me this much! I was proud to be his *protégé*.

When the second quarter started, it was the other team's ball. This time, when I stole the ball, I didn't think about my stomach. Instead, I simply passed the ball to Nick.

"That's what I'm talking about, David!" Coach hollered. I grinned.

Moments later, when the boy I was guarding attempted to score, I jumped up, hands over my head, and easily blocked his shot! I passed the ball to Peter who dribbled toward the foul line and then made a successful switch. The score was now 15 - 2. After Peter scored his shot, Coach Barry subbed Robby, Louis, and a couple of second graders in for everyone on the court except for Max.

"David, sit here," Coach Barry said, gesturing to the seat next to him. I did. He patted my back.

"I'm proud of you, buddy," he declared. "You bounced back and proved that I was right to trust you."

Just like that, a feeling of confidence filled me, and remained with me for the rest of the day.

By the time I was put back in, the score was 23 - 8. Two minutes later, as the team got into a stack, Coach Barry put the final sub into the game. By now we had all gotten playing time!

Soon after, Sam passed me the ball. I dribbled at top speed until I got near the basket and took my first shot of the game. It went in! The score was 25 - 8.

YES!! I felt redeemed for my mistake earlier, and my heart soared. I punched the air in triumph, feeling like I'd just lost a hundred dollars and found a thousand! I was in the *zone*. I continued making pass after pass, shot after shot, steal after steal. We ended up winning 32 - 13.

The tan-blue owl motif seemed to shimmer on Coach Barry's shirt as we all rushed together cheering.

"I'm very proud of you guys," Coach Barry shouted. "This was a great way to end the season. I hope you're all back next year. So, how many of you know Coach Jeff?" We all put our hands in the air. Coach Jeff coaches one of the more advanced basketball teams. In our town, our club basketball league is organized into four levels of teams: The Level 1 team, the Level 2, the Level 3 team, and the Level 4 team.

"Coach Jeff asked if I had any amazing players whom I think are ready to try out for his Level 2 team. I put seven of you on the list. Our official starters, plus David and Nick. And I think you all deserve it. Your skills are beyond those of most kids your age."

I was thrilled. He'd named me!

And can I tell you, that was nothing compared to the happy smiles on my parents' faces when I shared my great news with them. My parents had had such little joy for such a long time that their smiles made me feel better than a trip to Disney World!

In the Hole

3

Robbed!

At night, I struggled to rest. Living a Spartan life in a car, I was keenly aware that we were poor and in trouble. Still, life went on. Baseball season began. Mom had her birthday. To celebrate, we painted together at the house of a church friend, a nice lady who was in Mom's women's group. Dad and I painted pictures of baseball games. Julia painted horses. Mom's friend painted flowers. Mom painted a picture of the four of us outside a beautiful blue house with a big garden filled with blossoming flowers. My whole family got choked up when we saw Mom's picture.

Julia developed a cheerful hobby, picking wildflowers, or getting old unsellable flowers from the local florist and decorating our car with them.

Clearly, life was not all rainbows. My parents often got cranky. Who wouldn't? First of all, they had no space in their lives for romance. Who can flirt when you live in a tiny car with your kids? On top of that, the stress of not knowing whether they were going to be able to feed us, pay medical bills, or even keep us safe, was an enormous burden. They yelled at us at least twice a week for no apparent reason.

Eventually, another fateful day arrived. Like the day I lost my home, I was somewhere fun: Justin's birthday party. It was a baseball party, and we were all wearing blue and green t-shirts and playing our game in Justin's backyard, using mats as our bases and as a home plate.

We were playing against our parents, and everyone was enthusiastic and determined to win. My mom hadn't been able to come because she was meeting with my teacher to discuss how tired I had been in school.

"Of course, we all want to win," yelled Dad, laughing, "*But we're gonna' win!*"

"We'll show our parents how well they taught us," Justin advised as we huddled. "Lead-off batter and pitcher; Louis, you're next up and playing third base..." (I was sixth in the line-up and playing center field, my best position!) Justin went on, "And, guys, take no prisoners! We've gotta be as exceptional with our baseball skills as Joey Votto playing for the Reds!"

"Aye, aye, Captain!" Robby said. "In honor of your birthday, we'll be as militant as the actual military!" I smiled, patting Justin on the back.

"Good," said Justin. He wanted all of us to be good enough that we could be inducted into the Major League Baseball Hall of Fame! "It's going to be a challenge, considering how good certain parents of ours are. But we've got enough grit to *make it happen!*"

We looked at our parents. They seemed so confident and strong that it felt as if we were playing against MLB players! We knew it would be a daunting task to win against them.

"Justin, who's up first?" Max asked.

"We are," said Justin.

"And who's pitching?" asked Will, a slender Asian boy in fourth grade, whom Justin and I knew from our baseball league.

"Mrs. Gutierrez is," answered Justin as the parents took their places. "Now let's go, Louis!"

For a man whose son does not play baseball, Otto's mom was a pretty good pitcher. She even wound up his pitches—raising up her left leg and putting her whole body into her pitches. Boy, were they fast! Her first pitch smoked past Louis—*strike one.* Her next pitch was low—*ball one.* The next one was outside—*ball two.* Then she threw another one down the center of the plate and Louis swung with all his strength. It flew out to center field, where Mr. Lance scooped it up and threw it to Mr. Allen who was playing second base. He caught the ball just before Louis got to the base and Mr. Allen tagged him out. Next, Justin was up.

"Come on, Birthday Boy!" Eliot yelled. That must have made Justin nervous because he missed horribly—he swung before the ball even made it to the plate—*strike one.*

"You can do it!" I yelled. I wanted to show Justin as much support as he'd shown me since Dad lost his job. Justin stepped out of the batter's box and took a deep breath in and then let it out slowly. You could see him relax. Then he turned to look at us, smiled, and gave us a thumbs up. Then he got back into the batter's box. And this time he was ready. He swung at the next pitch and hit it over third base and into left field. By the time the ball was thrown back into the infield, Justin was standing on second base.

Will was third up. While he worked the count, he wasn't able to get a hit and struck out. Next was Nick. Mrs. Gutierrez threw a strike on the first pitch, then Nick hit the second one into short center field. It was deep enough that he was able to safely reach first base while Just ran to third.

Max was up next.

"Come on Max, just hit it deep enough to get Justin home," I called. "You're a baseball prodigy! It's time to let everyone know that!" Max nodded. Max hit the third pitch, a ground ball just outside of Mr. Allen's reach. It came to rest in short center field; still, it was deep enough for him to reach first base, Nick made it to second base, and Justin ran home! 1 - 0.

I was up next.

"COME ON, DAVID!" Justin yelled.

"You can do it!" hollered Otto.

I nodded hopefully. Taking a deep breath, I watched as Mrs. Gutierrez threw the ball at the center of the plate. I pulled my bat back and then swung it with all my strength and then *WHAM!* The ball flew all the way to the opposite side of the yard. Well over the head of Justin's aunt who was also Robby's mom, who was playing right field. By the time he got the ball and threw it back to the infield, I had already run the bases. A home run! Now, we were winning 4 - 0. It felt amazing.

Robby was up next. He hit the second pitch pretty far. Will's mom, however, at third base outfield, caught it.

Out!

The parents were up. Mr. O'Malley led off. He looked like a giant. Louis tried to throw the ball past him, then Mr. O'Malley pulled the bat back and let it rip and hit a home run. Will's dad was up next. He also almost hit it out. Then, Eliot, who was playing left field, jumped high and caught it.

"Nice, Eliot!" I cried, running over to give him a high five.

My dad was up next. I was tempted to smirk. *All the lessons you gave me on baseball are about to backfire, Dad—on you!* However, I was only half right. They did backfire—on *me*—since I had forgotten that my dad was fast and knew those lessons too! Like the two hitters before him, he swung at Louis' first pitch and hit right at me. By the time I ran it down, I could see that Dad was almost at second base and planning to run to third, so I threw it to Justin at third base. By the time Justin caught the ball, Dad was safe on third. Justin's mom hit a fast ball out to right field—far enough for him to safely reach second, more than far enough for Mr. Roberts to get to home plate—which he did. Next up, Otto's mom hit a home run.

"Come on, Louis," I shouted, "Throw some heat!"

Lucas nodded.

He pulled his arm way back and the fastball flew toward home plate. Otto's mom was up, and she hit a ground ball right to Will, who was playing shortstop. Will deftly caught the ball and tagged Mrs. Gutierrez as she was running to third, and then threw it to Sam at first base. Sam caught it. Double play!

"Great job, Will!" I yelled.

We were back up. Unfortunately, Eliot and Robby popped out. Then Justin's friend from camp, Steph Kulsiege, hit the ball out of the yard and into a neighbor's yard—automatic home run! We were now winning 5 - 4.

After that, the game turned into a defensive grind. Louis really brought his A-game, and even struck out some of the dads. Except for a couple of runs he gave up in the fourth inning, Louis basically shut the dads down for the rest of the game.

The problem was that we weren't doing any better. While we were getting runners on the bases, no one made it home. In the bottom of the ninth, the parents were still winning 6 – 5. There was one out and Max was standing on second base. I was up to bat. It's now or never, I thought. Mrs. Gutierrez threw the ball and, without thinking, I hit the ball with all my strength. It flew out of the yard and into the neighbor's yard—another home run! 7 - 6! *We won!* I had never felt so supercharged in my life! My teammates ran toward me.

"MVP!" Justin yelled.

"MVP!"

"Great job, David!" Max added, as we crowded into Justin's house for birthday cake.

Within minutes, I was in for a shock. Mom arrived in tears.

"David! Harry!" she whispered when she reached me and my dad. "Something terrible has happened!"

What unfolded next shook me to the core, and left me devastated.

"What happened, Charlotte?" Dad asked. Mom suddenly dragged us toward the door.

"Come on, we have to go now. David, please just leave your baseball bat, cap, and glove here."

Okay. Those are weird instructions, I thought. I apologized and said goodbye to Justin, wished him a happy birthday, and left with my parents. As we reached the church parking lot, my heart sank...

The spot where our car had been was empty.

"*Wh-where's* our car!?" I squealed.

"Oh honey, it was stolen!" replied Mom, falling to her knees and sobbing. She wept and wept. Dad's face was very serious.

"Charlotte, did you call the police?" he asked. Mom let out a heavy sigh.

"I called the Jeffers—since it was their car we borrowed—and they reported it to the police, while I listened in on the line. They will report back to the Jeffers if it is found."

My self-esteem was waning by the second. I was furious! That car may have been tiny and gross. Even so, it was the closest thing to a home that I had at the moment! In fact, I was angry enough that I wanted to find the thief as quickly as possible and bash his head on the ground a million times!

I suddenly realized that Julia wasn't there with us. "Did they kidnap Julia?" I asked, terrified.

Mom shook her head. "I didn't want her to see this so I arranged for her to go home with Ella after her riding lesson." Ella, who is a couple of years older than Julia, is her best friend. I heard my mother mutter, "Thank God Julia can still ride for free and do something she loves. It's about the only thing that hasn't been taken from us."

"Can she stay with Ella until we find a shelter?" I asked. Mom nodded. "Ella's parents already agreed to that," she informed us. Tears dropped from her eyes.

"Charlotte?" Concerned, Dad reached for Mom.

Mom took my dad's hand.

"*Wh-where are we going to go?*" I whispered.

"I'm not sure," Mom replied, "Trust, my darling, that no matter what, we will be safe, David. Don't worry."

Sleeping without any shelter would be a nightmare. Standing in that church parking lot facing our life as it was that day, my dignity 100% ruined—in the drizzling rain—I'm ashamed to admit that in that moment, I truly wished I had never been born. I also began to feel very cynical about religion. Up until that point, like my parents, I had been a strong, proud churchgoer. But why would God have allowed such a horrible fate to befall us!? And *why should I try to be a good Christian and do what God wants, if He is just going to let people steal my family's car and make us sleep in the rain?*

That night, we somehow managed to camp in the woods behind our church. It was the most uncomfortable place I had ever slept. I was freezing and miserable (so were Mom and Dad), and I could not stop crying.

The next day, we went to church where they let us take showers before services began. However, instead of feeling grateful, I felt humiliated and resentful that I had to lean on the church to shower, and about everything that had happened. I'm not proud of this; during the service, I actually prayed for the thief to die as painful a death as possible before I heard my mother's voice in my head saying, "God doesn't want anyone praying for anyone else's death." At the time, though, I honestly didn't care.

I was plotting ways to find and attack said thief when Mom, Dad, and I went to the O'Malley's house for lunch. Justin wrapped me up in a big bro hug the minute he saw me.

"Oh my God, David, you look terrible! What happened?"

"I slept in the rain in the woods behind our church." I said, looking down at my sneakers. My anger was obvious. *They say April showers bring May flowers? Well, May showers don't bring a happy David Kimball!* I thought. Looking him straight in the eye, I told Justin, "Some idiot that I'm super mad at likes to steal cars." For an hour, we talked about ways to get revenge on the thief.

When we finally joined our parents, Mrs. O'Malley was telling mine about a nearby, slightly run-down inn here in the Southwest area of Wood Creek. "Its owner renovated it into housing for people who lost their homes," she explained, and offered, "We could take you to see the man who owns the inn. He works at the front desk."

"That would be great," Mom said.

Justin handed me a really amazing Reds jersey. "This is a facsimile of George Foster's jersey," he said.

"Oh yeah!" I exclaimed. "You won it at that competition for most home runs when we were in first grade!"

"Well. It's yours now," said Justin. "You need something dry."

"Justin, I don't think that's a good idea! You earned it!"

"David, I don't care. You need it more," he insisted.

"Thanks, Justin," I replied. I put it on, smiling gratefully.

Thirty minutes later, after we had helped the O'Malleys clean up the mess from Justin's party, they took us to the old inn that our parents had been talking about. An older man with a mop of curly red hair and dimples, stood at the front desk. He wore a professional button-down shirt and trousers. The adults leaned in to talk to him. Justin and I stood and watched baseball on a crappy old television in the equally crappy waiting area.

"Thanks again for lending me your shirt, Justin," I said. "I know it's worth a lot of money on eBay, so it's really generous of you to trust me with it."

Justin shrugged and gave me a really nice nonchalant reply, "It depends on how you look at it, David. You needed a new shirt, so why not give you something even better? You're my best friend, after all." I knew how lucky I was to be best friends with Justin!

My parents and the O'Malleys finished talking to the gentleman at the inn's desk and called us over.

"Wonderful news! We're moving in tonight!" Mom explained. "I just paid for the first month."

I was confused. *The place must be cheap,* I thought, *if my mom's wallet money can pay for it.*

"Where did you get the money, Mom?" I asked.

"I had a couple hundred rainy day dollars saved before we lost everything," Mom explained.

"The inn allows people and families who have lost their homes to stay here for a very small amount of money, for as long as they need to. We're lucky my purse was not in our old car," she added with a wink. (Little did I know my mom had been taking on housekeeping jobs to help keep us afloat.)

"Justin," Mrs. O'Malley asked, "could you lend David a sleeping bag and some clothes? And give him a fresh toothbrush from the bathroom cupboard."

"Sure," said Justin. He turned to me. "Do you want me to give you a baseball and a basketball?" (Along with my sleeping bag and other worldly possessions, my baseball had been in the car when it was stolen.)

"Thanks, bro," I replied, grinning.

While Justin and I gathered clothes together, Mom and Mrs. O'Malley went to grab some supplies from the grocery store and pick up Julia from Ella's. The inn already had furniture; nevertheless, my mom wanted us to have four chairs. So the O'Malleys also loaned us their spares, along with a small table. I was super grateful because every piece of furniture, whether it was old or not, was a true gift. As far as I was concerned, nothing could be taken for granted anymore.

Our room at the inn was cold, even in May. The windows had wood frames, and it was very easy for the wind to get into the space. Our inn room was small. We had the little round table and chairs lent to us by the O'Malleys, and we each slept in a sleeping bag on a small futon in a different corner of the room, with Mom and Dad sharing a corner. The futons doubled as couches during the day. In the fourth corner was a built-in kitchen space where my parents could cook with whatever food we had on hand. It wasn't much, yet it sure beat living in our car.

That first night at the inn I felt grateful to be snug in Justin's old synthetic trophy shirt inside Justin's sleeping bag. That sleeping bag was also a family treasure (it had belonged to Justin's great grandfather who had used it camping). I felt warm, cozy, and grateful for my generous friend. I was thankful to be sleeping neither in a car nor on the street; at last, we were in a safe, heated, old house occupied by at least a dozen homeless people—and my family—all down on our luck.

4

The Truth Comes Out

One way that Julia and I were different from one another was that Julia was not ashamed of the fact that we were destitute.

Once, we were at the supermarket and Julia ran into her best friend, Ella. The plainly dressed man who ran the inn was there, too. Ella overheard Julia say hi to him.

"You know *him*?" Ella asked incredulously.

"Yeah, he's my friend," was Julia's innocent reply.

I never would have told that to *anyone*—other than to Justin of course. What if people started asking how *I* knew the old man from the inn? The way I saw it, I was worthless because I was homeless. I devalued myself 100%. Even so, I did not want others to look down on me—or worse, to pity me.

Then one day, as fate would have it, my mom took me fishing at a nearby lake with Otto, Peter, and Sam, and the man from the inn was fishing at the water's edge. I recognized his plain attire even though he wasn't wearing a button-down like he usually did. From where he stood setting up his fishing gear, I saw him glancing over at me several times.

At a certain point, he waved and called out to me, "Hi, David!" A few seconds later, he tried again. "Hey, David!" And finally, "David! Hello!" *Three times he tried to get my attention.* I am still ashamed to admit refused to answer. I just pretended not to hear him at all.

"Who's *that* dude?" Otto had asked and I shrugged.

"Hope he stops yelling, 'cause he's scaring the fish away," Sam had remarked, casting his reel again.

That night, I got a pretty good scolding from Mom!

Another time I was also confronted with my shame. During the first week of summer vacation I came home from baseball practice to find Julia having a playdate with three of her cowgirl friends at the inn. My brain was on fire!

"Julia," I sputtered, trying not to sound too angry, "why didn't you ask my permission?!"

Outraged, Julia whirled around, almost dropping the stuffed horse she was holding.

"*Your* permission, David? First you yell at me for mentioning our address to Shannon. Then, I asked Mom if the Cowgirls could have a sleepover here with me and you burst out *No!* And now you tell me I need your *permission* to have my besties over? You are *not* the boss of me!" Julia finished, scathingly.

I felt my face burn red as I tried not to feel frustrated and ashamed. All I could think was, *How can I explain to my five-year-old sister that our "home" is something to be ashamed of, something to cause people to consider us losers?*

Of course, Mom overheard the altercation.

"Dave, can we talk outside?" I nodded. Mom took me outside and asked, "Are you down on yourself because we are struggling right now, sweetheart?" I nodded.

"I'm scared that if Julia's friends—or *my* friends—know that we're homeless, that they'll judge us and gossip about us."

"I can understand that, sweetheart." Mom nodded compassionately. "I don't think Julia's friends—even the ones who have siblings you are friends with—will think to tell your friends about our living situation." I stared at my sneakers. Mom continued. "Julia still has her self-esteem, honey. She's too young to understand that we are homeless. As long as we are all together, Julia considers wherever we live like a home. I think you should let her keep her self-esteem and stop worrying about her friends—and yours—being aware of where we live. Okay?"

I nodded. My feelings of anger and caring about my reputation immediately changed to a feeling of wanting to protect my sister.

"Okay, Mom. Okay."

The summer was long and uneventful. I got used to the inn. Whenever I was home, I was usually sitting in my family's room reading at the O'Malleys' round table, or in the tiny corner of our room where I slept. Julia and Mom both tried to use whatever material we had left over in boxes to make outfits. Some turned out well. Most, however, pretty much just revealed the fact we were homeless. Mom also spent a lot of time painting. Even though there wasn't a lot of rain that summer, Mom painted a lot of pictures of rainy days. I think the rain symbolized her depression about our situation. She also painted quite a few pictures of the Crucifixion.

Even during the heatwave that summer, Julia continued to ride horses at the free program. And as usual, Julia's equestrian events required a special wardrobe. Plus, Julia was quickly outgrowing her jodhpurs and the purple velvet show coat Mom and Dad had given her for her birthday the year before. Fortunately, Ella lent Julia her outgrown riding habit. For her sixth birthday, Julia and her friends went for ice cream in town. For that, my mom sold some of her jewelry on eBay.

Summer found my gregarious dad spending a lot of time gathering information about Wayne Gretzky and playing football, basketball, and baseball with the dads of my friends and Julia's friends in the evenings and on weekends. Sometimes when he played with my friends' dads, my friends and I would join them. Mostly, I spent my days at Justin's, playing sports or video games with him, and "eating us out of house and home," as Justin's mom teased. In fact, the O'Malleys never made me feel anything but welcome.

That autumn, the first day of fourth grade began pretty well. I'd already met my teacher, Mrs. Swanson. Just like in third grade, we had a seatmate, and mine was Nick! After being seated with girls for all of third grade, it felt nice to finally be seatmates with one of my friends. Nick and I mostly talked about our summers.

I will admit it was confounding, even infuriating, being ashamed of my home situation when Julia was not. During about the third weekend of school, she had two sleepovers at the inn, and I felt more frustrated than ever! (If you are wondering how we had room for her buddies, the weather was still warm enough for them to sleep outside on the grass by the lake in their sleeping bags!) Then one day, things happened that started an avalanche of trouble for me. Eliot and I were taking a bike ride after school and talking about the changes to our class. Eventually, I looked at my watch.

"Eliot, I have to go," I said. "Mom insists my homework is always finished by five on weeknights."

"Could I come to your house with you?" Eliot asked.

By now, I was used to saying no.

"Sorry, it's a busy time."

"David, c'mon. I haven't been to your new house!" Eliot protested.

"You just always ask at bad times!" I snapped as I biked away.

Little did I know Eliot was secretly following me.

The next day, at lunch, when I came out to join my friends, they all gave me weird looks.

"Um, what's going on?" I asked nervously.

"I followed you to that inn and asked the front desk dude if you lived there!" Eliot announced indignantly. "You've been living there for months and keeping it a secret from us!"

"I can't believe you lied to us!" Max yelled.

"I-I never said I wasn't!" I said nervously.

"Doesn't matter. Keeping it a secret is the same thing as lying!" Robby concurred.

"I agreed to let Justin tell *you*, Robby!" I protested. Justin gave me an apologetic look.

"I decided it wasn't my place to let him know," Justin whispered.

"Wait a minute! Justin knew?" Nick asked.

"You've only known Justin since you were six! I've known you longer!" exclaimed Otto angrily. *That was super low!* I thought.

"Justin's my bestie, Otto!" I protested. "You know that! Ask yourself these two questions: One, if *you* were homeless, would you tell *me*? And two, if you were homeless, would you tell Nick and Max?"

Otto's dark brown eyes flashed with anger as he knocked me to the ground. He only needed one push, because he was a lot taller and stronger than I was, especially since I had been eating so little for so many months.

Eliot glared at me. "I thought we were friends," he said angrily, "Friends tell each other the truth. Tell me, David, what else have you been hiding from us? Have you been stealing food?"

"Yeah," said Max. "You're not my friend anymore!"

"Or mine!" said Nick.

"Or mine!" the rest of the guys except Justin said in unison.

I could not believe how mean and unfair and immature my friends were being! At that moment, I felt years older, like a broken old man.

"Fine," I said, feeling really angry and hurt. I stood up straight and tall—well, as tall as I could stand (especially in that moment, I *hated* being short!). "Since you guys think I'm a liar, you should feel fortunate you'll never have to see me again!"—which of course was impossible since we were all in the same school.

I ran all the way to the inn with angry tears pouring from my eyes. I figured I had probably lost Louis, Sam, Will, and Peter as well. They, too, would most likely be mad that I hadn't told them the truth. I felt really upset— upset at Dad, for not being careful when he hired a drug addict, upset at the fact we were homeless, and upset at my friends for being so unkind! *They don't care about me!* I convinced myself.

When I got to the inn, my legs were so tired that I almost wanted them amputated.

"Why can't houses be free?" I sobbed as I flew into the room where Mom was working on that oil painting of our family in front of a blue house.

Mom immediately dropped her paint brush in the jar of turpentine and ran over to embrace me. "Honey, what's wrong? Why aren't you in school?"

I told her everything. "I'm not going back." I declared. "I've lost all my friends."

"Even Justin?" Mom asked.

"There are going to be days when he's not in school, Mom," I pointed out. "And I can't predict when those days will be."

Mom considered my predicament for a few minutes while she continued to hug me.

"Okay," she finally said, "Let's go to the Public Library and you can grab some books about math, science, and language arts."

"What?" I was caught off guard.

"Yes, I'll homeschool you personally," my mother reassured me.

(My mom was wise enough to know a few "mental health days" at home alone with Mom and Dad, 24/7, would soon make me crave the company of my schoolmates.)

A week later, I was reading a book about value digits in the library, when I heard someone sneak up behind me.

"Hi, Dave."

I turned around, surprised and ecstatic to see my best friend. "Hey, Justin," I said, giving him a fist-bump.

Justin looked at what I was reading. "You hate math! I thought you only liked to read about sports!" We both laughed.

"I'm dropping out of school," I told him. "I'll continue studying, though."

"Dave, you can't just drop out," Justin protested. "It's not the same in class without you."

"It's too much pressure on *you* that I feel I need you in school every single day no matter what," I told Justin. "And I don't want to be at school alone with a pack of guys against me."

Justin rolled his dark brown eyes. "David," he told me firmly, "after you ran off, I gave the guys a huge talk and they all feel terrible about what they said, especially Eliot. If you come back to school, I'm sure they'll apologize."

I thought for a moment. It was obvious Justin really wanted me to come back, and he never lied to me.

"Okay," I said, "I'll come back." I decided not to be angry at my friends for not having a good reaction when they found out about me being homeless. They were my friends and besides, my mother always said that the best relationships were built on forgiveness.

As I walked to school the next day, Justin's father's black Jeep drove up alongside me. Justin rolled down his window.

"Get in, David! You're coming with us."

I grinned and climbed in. When we arrived at school, Justin gathered all the other boys; they were exchanging glances nervously.

"Dudes, is there anything you want to say to Dave?" Justin prompted. They nodded.

Robby was the first to reach his hand out. "I'm sorry about what I said, David," he said.

"Thanks," I murmured and shook his hand.

One by one, the other guys apologized, as well. It was hard and awkward, but I forgave them. What was the point of staying angry? It made me feel tired. And, after all, they knew what they did was wrong.

That weekend, for the first time, Justin and I had a sleepover at the inn. Justin's parents generously sent along food with him so my mom wouldn't have to worry about using too much of my family's supply.

"If you don't mind my saying so, David, the inn room is actually kind of pretty," Justin told me after he arrived in our room. He glanced around. "The light blue walls make the room feel like the ocean surrounding some kind of warm cozy submarine. And those chairs are super comfortable," he added glancing at the silver chairs that his family had given us. "Back when these chairs belonged to my family, I always felt like a king when I sat in them."

Justin looked at the corner of the room where his great grandfather's sleeping bag was rolled up on my futon. It was surrounded by books from the Public Library by my favorite author, Mike Lupica, such as *Heat*, *Summer Ball*, and *Safe at Home*, and a recent one called *Hero*. There was also my sports equipment, notebooks, and even a pair of posters about my favorite *Superman* video game. It was like all of the different sections of my old bedroom had become one crowded corner.

"And you never have to reach that far to get anything if you need something to do," Justin added.

I rolled my eyes. "I get it, Justin. You like the inn. Trust me, it's still not as good as having a big house."

Justin shrugged. "It's not that great living in a big mansion anyway," he told me. "The first time I went to Otto's house, because of its gigantic size, I ended up getting lost!" I giggled. I knew Justin was trying to make me feel better. "We could have a potluck party here, Dave."

"We?" I asked. Justin nodded. "You, me, and the gang."

"Only if my riding squad can come," Julia butted in.

"No, Julia, we aren't inviting your friends from horseback riding," I told her firmly. Julia shrugged as she pulled her curly brown hair into a ponytail.

"If you say so," she said. Then, looking at her hairbrush and comb lying on a nearby table she offered, "Justin, do you want me to do your hair before you go to bed?"

"No, thanks, Julia," said Justin. "But it's kind of you to ask."

We went outside to play catch for fifteen minutes until it got dark. After that, we stayed inside with my family and I began to feel more comfortable. Perhaps Justin had a point that the inn wasn't that bad a place. It wasn't as great as my old house. Still, I knew I should make the most of what I had.

5

David Kimball, Businessman

Not everything about our life at the inn was awful. For example, in addition to being a haven for folks who found themselves homeless, the inn itself was actually quite okay looking, as were the surrounding yards. There was also a lake nearby that was clean in which Justin and I swam a lot that summer. There were a bunch of apple trees, too, and some of the rooms, ours included, even had flower boxes attached to the windowsills with a few flowers growing inside. In ours, we discovered a bright beautiful potted red rose that my mom moved to our table. Looking at the flower had made being stuck in the tiny room of the inn feel better. It's funny, when there are beautiful things around, they can actually put you in a good mood.

In October 2010, about four weeks after my friends found out I was homeless, Max and I took a bike ride around the inn parking lot and along some little trails in the woods that were part of the property. As we biked, Max and I talked happily the way nine-year-old boys do and told each other jokes.

"What does a British vampire say after he bites you?" Max asked. I shrugged. *"Bloody sorry."* I had to admit that one was pretty good.

"How's soccer season going, Max?"

"Pretty good," Max replied. "I have a game tomorrow. If my team wins, it'll put us in the lead for the championship." I gave him a fist-bump.

"Win tomorrow. Okay, man?" I told him.

Max nodded. "Okay, David. You know you can count on me."

We biked a while longer until we reached the far end of the parking lot. There, we came upon what looked from a distance like a giant anthill. That was weird. Approaching it closely, we saw what it really was—a bunch of toys, books, clothes, and pieces of furniture, all covered by a large plastic tarp.

"Look at all this stuff!" Max said excitedly, picking up a tattered copy of *Green Eggs and Ham*. "Think of the money we could make selling all of it," Max said dreamily.

Wait a minute. *Money? Money? Money?!* That was it! I could sell some of this stuff and maybe, after some time, earn enough to help my family have a house again!

"Max!" I exclaimed. "You're a genius!"

"I am?" Max asked.

"Yup," I laughed. "You just gave me a great idea! C'mon, let's grab a few things and then we can go back to my inn room."

"Okay," said Max.

Quickly, I grabbed *The Moosewood Cookbook* for Mom, a Reds uniform for Dad, and a stuffed swan to give to Julia. Then, Max and I rode back to the inn.

Later that day, after Max had gone home, I went to talk to Mr. Jamison, the plainly dressed man who owned the inn.

"Hi, David, what can I do for you?" he asked. I told him about the pile of stuff Max and I had found. The man's mustache twitched. "Ah, yes. That stuff came from former inn residents who couldn't take everything with them when they found permanent housing or moved to other states to find work. They left those possessions behind and I put the stuff at the back of the inn for safe keeping and covered it all with a tarp to try to keep it clean and dry." Mr. Jamison paused a moment, thinking. "What did you have in mind?"

"Well, I was wondering, Mr. Jamison, if it might be okay if I sell some of that stuff to raise money for my family?" I asked.

After stroking his mustache several times, Mr. Jamison nodded. "I think that is a very clever idea, David." Music to my ears! "To tell you the truth, David, that pile of things has become an eye sore. And I don't believe anyone who left those things behind will ever come to reclaim them."

That night, inside my family's room, I grabbed a cardboard box, pulled off one of the sides, and wrote on it in huge letters, *THE DAVID KIMBALL YARD SALE!* Mom was in our room sipping tea and re-stitching one of Julia's old stuffed animals that was falling apart. When she noticed the pile of stuff I had brought back for everyone, she came over curiously to see what I was writing out in such huge letters.

"What's all this?" she asked, perplexed.

"Mom," I replied smiling, "I am going to get us out of poverty."

That evening, by flashlight and with four sturdy trash bags, I went back to the pile of abandoned stuff and bagged up as much as I could. I also found two bamboo poles. I considered asking Dad for help, but my pride got to me. I wanted to be independent and raise some money on my own. With all of the strength I had, I dragged everything back to the inn room and left it on the back porch. After that, I went back and grabbed folding chairs and some other light pieces of furniture from the pile. Unfortunately, I wasn't strong enough to carry beds, tables, or any other types of bigger furniture. Those would've been great to sell; still I had a ton of saleable stuff.

After school the next day, I organized everything into groups—clothing, toys, books, etc. Mr. Jamison had been watching me from the main door to the inn. Eventually he came out to see if he could lend a hand, and kindly helped me set up a sign next to the road. When Mr. Jamison returned to his desk, I organized everything in the parking lot in front of the inn before calling Justin and a few other friends and asking them to tell their neighbors about the sale and to please come see if they needed any of the cool and useful items.

No one came that night, even though I sat outside waiting until the sun set and my stomach began to growl. Eventually, my mom called me in for dinner. So, I gave up for the night, covering everything up and going inside to be with my family. It was a good start.

The next day, when I arrived home from school, I found a number of people standing around the parking lot of the inn looking kind of confused, as no one seemed to be running the sale. I recognized some of the people from the inn, and others were complete strangers. Many of those gathered seemed interested in buying some of the things that I had set out. I made a note to myself that I would need to make signs saying *Open* and *Closed*.

Quickly, I got behind the pay stand and announced, "The yard sale is open!"

Everyone clapped and cheered.

"How much for this chair?" A man asked, carrying a black chair with an orange cushion.

"Eleven dollars," I replied, beaming. (I had set the prices based on how much I personally estimated the thing to be worth. That orange cushion looked really comfy!) I don't know what it is about business, everyone loves to have their first customer.

A woman picked up a blue teapot and three teacups and asked for a price.

"Eight dollars and fifty cents," I said.

A teenager asked for a shirt with a cat on it. A mother asked for a stuffed toy puppy for her son. A kid between Julia's age and mine bought a pair of my old basketball shoes. This was wonderful! I had about nineteen customers that day, including Louis from my basketball team, his parents, and my mom's friend from her church club, Mrs. Swanson. There was also an elderly couple from the inn, the Watsons. They were both very friendly and wore awesome matching gray Batman t-shirts. We had a quick conversation about Justice League together before they bought an old coffee machine. (The Watsons eventually become friends with my parents.)

By the end of the day, I had earned one hundred and five dollars!

When I handed a wad of cash to my parents that night, they could not believe their eyes!

"David, this is wonderful!" exclaimed Mom, her hazel eyes widening. "Please, sweetie, don't give all of this money to your father and me."

"You need it!" I protested. Had Mom lost her mind? She shook her head firmly.

"You earned all this money holding a yard sale when you aren't even ten years old yet! It's only right that you spend some of it on something special for yourself."

"Please, please, Mom," I insisted, "take at least seventy-five dollars. It might be the only money I'm able to give you for a while—at least until I find another way to earn it. I wasn't sure how long it would take me to find another way to make money. I also could not believe that my own mother, a person without a home, would or should refuse any amount of money!

Mom thought for a moment. "How about a compromise, David? I'll take eighty dollars and you get to spend the rest on a treat for yourself." That seemed fair.

"Okay," I shrugged. How the heck could Mom be that selfless when we didn't even have a home?

Meanwhile, my parents were looking for ways to earn money too. They had been searching for jobs for months ever since we lost our home. Mom and Dad were both emailing every business they could in order to find a job. They also went door to door asking for work at all the businesses downtown, and in the more prosperous neighborhoods. However, finding a job was hard, even when you went door-to-door, business-to-business, asking if you can be paid to do any kind of odd job. There weren't a lot of places hiring in Wood Creek, and many people had not forgotten how Dad's restaurant had closed because of the kidnapping by Dad's weird employee, Mr. Hawthorne.

Employers told Dad, basically, "You mean well, but your record shows you to be unreliable and irresponsible. We don't want any kidnapping at our establishment."

That frustrated me beyond what I can say. Dad made one mistake and that ruined his entire future?! It was too unfair.

Mom sometimes found part-time work doing housekeeping or small painting jobs. Those usually only lasted for a week or two. Eventually, in November, Mom began to cook daily for the mother of Alexa Brewer, the girl from my class who loved to bully me. Even though I knew we needed money, I felt humiliated. For the entire month of November, Alexa was my seatmate and rubbed in the *fact* that my mom was her mom's *servant* and that her family was *better* than mine. It took all the guts I had to ignore her.

Even worse, after months of constant struggle and rejection, Dad quit trying to find a job. He was caught in a downward spiral of depression, frustration, and anxiety, and began to swipe money from Mom and friends and God-knows-where-else and secretly go to a pub outside of Wood Creek. At the pub he met a few unsavory types, men who spent all their time drinking alcohol, gambling, and going to fast food restaurants. Dad became friends with them, and they were more than happy to pay for his fast food and booze. Dad began to drink with them on a nightly basis, often not returning home until three or four in the morning.

In the weeks following his decision to stop job-hunting, my father's behavior changed dramatically. Before we lost our home, Dad was one of the coolest people I knew. He was very smart and loved to collect information about athletes. In fact, I'm sure I get my love of sports from him. Before things got so bad, my dad wasn't afraid to try new things. He played sports with me, and at one point, ages earlier, he even tried to learn how to tap dance! I will never forget the time my second-grade teacher held a ball for all the parents, and he completely embarrassed Mom by tap dancing in the middle of the floor while everyone else waltzed.

In the old days, Dad went rock climbing, coached high school sports, and did a bunch of other really neat things. He was also super friendly and got along easily with most everyone. He would swap jokes and play catch with me and my friends, and he would talk about horses with Julia and her equestrian pals. Dad also looked awfully cool. Even though I am short, my dad stands six foot four. He also had long muscular arms, rippling abs, rock-star-long brown hair, intense green eyes, and a winning smile.

Dad was good at making other people feel better about themselves. He helped my mom, for example, to gain more confidence. As beautiful as she is with her hazel eyes and sweet smile, my mom was actually very shy as a child and self-conscious about being short (she was five foot two). But my dad made her feel like she was the most special person in the world.

These days, unfortunately, it seemed like Dad had given up. He was just not the same person. He was aggressive and moody. He didn't exercise much, and he ate a lot more—mostly fast food that his unsavory friends paid for when they went out—and he was going from six-pack to obese. When he was home, which was hardly ever, he also watched a lot more television than Julia and I had ever seen him watch. He stopped cooking pretty much altogether, though that had been his passion. Mom, of course, was horrified by his new attitude and lifestyle. They often spent hours arguing; she would beg him to stop drinking and spending time with his gutter-level friends. Then, Dad would just insist he needed a "retreat."

One night, in early November, I woke up at midnight to see Dad walk in with two of these unsavory types. They had long overgrown mustaches and smelled like whiskey, and they were carrying a lot of money. (When my mom saw that Dad was carrying quite a bit of cash too, I heard her whisper in horror to herself, "Please tell me Harry has not started dealing drugs.") The men also carried heavy knives which stuck out of their pockets.

Mom gasped in shock, before hissing venomously, "Get your drunken friends out of here right *now* and don't let me catch you bringing them into this inn again, *Harrison!*" Her cheeks flushed bright with anger.

Dad rolled his eyes and grunted, "Don't tell me who I can hang out with, Charlotte!"

"Hush! No, Harry, I am *not* letting you expose the children to these bad influences you hang out with. Oh my God—the children." Mom whipped her head around to look at Julia and me in our sleeping bags. "Thank God, they are not awake." Julia was still sleeping. My eyes, however, were wide open. Then, Mom clasped a hand over her mouth and gasped. Turning back to Dad, she hissed again, "David's awake, Harry! Get these men out *now*!"

"You have a son?" The smaller one of Dad's two friends asked curiously. He came over to where I was now sitting up in my sleeping bag and he crouched down next to me. The stench of his whiskey breath made me wrinkle my nose. I could barely breathe through it. The man picked up my copy of *Million Dollar Throw* and told me, "Why do you have all of these books. Reading is a waste of time and school gets you nowhere! I dropped out of high school and look how successful I am!" He flashed some dollars at me.

At this, my mom had had enough. She picked up the sharpest knife she could find in our silverware drawer and pointed it at the two men. I was shocked. My mom was the least violent person I'd ever met. I never thought I'd see her threaten someone with a knife. But she would do anything to protect Julia and me.

"How dare you talk to my son?!" she snapped. "Get out of here *now*!"

The two men slunk away and once they were out of the inn, Mom closed the door and locked it. Once the door was locked, Mom ran over and hugged me.

"David," Mom said softly—sternly—as if I had better believe her, "You are having a nightmare. It is time to dream happy dreams. Sweet dreams." She kissed my head and waited for me to lie down and get comfortable before she turned back to Dad and commanded, "Harrison, we are going outside to talk about your atrocious lifestyle—*now!*" She grabbed Dad's hand and led him outside to the porch.

The next morning, after that shaky evening, I spent the first few hours riding my bike in the woods near the inn, trying to clear my brain. As I rode around on the edge of the property, I saw various people who were also living at the inn taking walks, mowing a lawn, and throwing a ball for a dog. I realized that there were many stories unfolding all around me. Suddenly I remembered that my cousin had given me a video camera for my last birthday. What if I used the camera to help tell their stories to raise money? After all, the yard sale had been a huge success. Why couldn't I find additional ways to raise money for my family? I gave this more thought during the day and by evening I had decided to make a mini-documentary about life at the inn called *Life Goes On*. I decided to interview my family and friends who had visited our room at the inn, as well as some of the people I had met at the inn, including Mr. Jamison.

During the next week I interviewed Mom, who described a life full of tears and pain trying to get enough food for Julia, me, Dad, and herself. She also expressed how hard it was to keep such a small place tidy and showed me some of her paintings. "The reason I made the sky black in this picture is to emphasize just how dark things feel for me and my family," she explained showing me a picture with a pitch-black sky. I also interviewed Justin about hanging out with me at the inn.

My interview with my father was a disaster and led to another breakdown within our family. One day, I tried to interview Dad while Julia was out riding, and Mom was at a friend's house. I made the mistake of attempting this while my father was watching television. In those days, he watched so much TV that I didn't think he would mind being interrupted.

I was very wrong.

"Mr. Kimball," I asked, "what can you tell me about being homeless?"

"David, shut up," snapped my father.

I ignored him, and continued filming. "As I was saying, what can—?"

"Didn't you hear me, David Kimball—?"

"Dad, please—"

"Go away!"

"But—"

Dad grabbed my video camera right from my hands and threw it across the room. It hit the wall and crashed to the floor. I picked it up and saw at once that the screen was completely shattered—as was my heart.

I'd saved my earlier interviews with Mom and Justin onto Mom's phone. Obviously, now I could not shoot anymore, however. I blinked back tears as I looked at my father. This was not the man who had raised me. I would be ten in a month and had known this man my whole life, and yet up until now, I'd never seen him lose it! Completely controlled by alcohol, he'd gone insane. I felt terrified.

"Run!" a voice in my head told me. *Where?* I wondered. Justin's house, the voice told me. *What if I don't make it?* Justin's family lived at least six streets away. To me in that moment, the distance did not matter even though I was terrified; I knew I had to give it a try!

I raced out of the inn as fast as I could. It took me twenty minutes to run to O'Malley's. When I arrived, I was as breathless as I was upset.

Mrs. O'Malley looked aghast.

"David! Are you okay?"

"N-no!" I whimpered, "S-something's wr-wrong with my dad!"

Just then Justin entered the kitchen." Mom, did you say David—? Oh!" The sight of his mother giving me a hug surprised him.

Seeing the tears rolling down my cheeks, Justin asked, "Dave, you okay? You look like your puppy got run over!"

Concerned, he brought me into his living room and had me sit on the couch. That felt good. Justin's living room was super comfortable and had some of the coziest chairs I've ever sat on. I continued crying as I told Justin what had happened.

"I never saw Dad lose control before! The sight of it is—really frightening!"

"Do you want to stay here tonight, David?" Justin asked.

"Yes, please," I replied. "I just need to call my mom."

Justin's mom was already on the phone talking to mine! Mrs. O'Malley came walking into the living room with her cellphone pressed to her ear.

"He's okay, Charlotte, I think. He and Justin are talking." She handed me her phone.

"Mom?" I forced down the lump in my throat.

"David, listen to me for a minute. I heard about your fight with Dad. I want you to know I'm really sorry Dad lost control and that I'll buy you a new video camera. In return, I ask you to forgive your father. He is struggling with a terrible addiction and he needs our love right now. Though I understand it isn't easy after what happened. And running to the O'Malleys for help was a really smart idea. I am always going to be proud of you."

I was amazed at just how much could come out of Mom's mouth.

"Could I sleep over at Justin's tonight? I could use a few hours away from Dad." I asked quickly.

"Sure, of course you can. I understand," replied Mom.

After Mom hung up, Justin and I played basketball. Later we watched *Batman: Under the Red Hood*. However, Justin did not have to be a genius to realize I was still upset. It was impossible for me to get my mind off what had happened. First, Justin beat me 28 - 4 on the court. On a normal day, that would never happen. I'd always been better than Justin at basketball. Second, when Justin and I talked about *Batman* after we were done watching it, I barely knew what we were talking about. Because I loved movies, that was also incredibly unusual.

"Dave, are you okay?" Justin asked that night.

"I'm kind of overwhelmed, Justin," I replied. "What happened really frightened me."

"You should talk to your Dad," Justin told me. "It might help." Justin then told me about a time when he was six. He'd been in a car with his dad and his brother Eric, while the two of them were arguing. Mr. O'Malley was completely out of control with anger, and he had almost left Eric out on the street. "But Eric and my father made up, David. You and your dad can too!"

I nodded and went to bed early. I spent that night praying. I knew I had to forgive Dad. We all have difficult days.

The next day, when I got home, I saw my father watching TV.

"Wait for him to finish," Mom told me.

When Dad finally shut off the television, he saw me, and held out his hand.

"I'm sorry I lost it last night, buddy," said Dad.

"It's okay," I replied shaking his hand. I still felt cautious. I was not sure I could trust him yet. And boy, was I relieved that *that* episode seemed to be over.

By December, using a secondhand video camera Mom had bought me from the pawn shop, and editing the footage on her phone, I had enough interviews to make a mini-movie—including one autobiographical scene! I showed it to my mom, and she loved it. I felt super proud. If I was lucky, maybe the local movie theater would like it just as much. (A boy could hope!) Although Dad still wouldn't let me interview him, I did interview Julia and a few of our friends.

Plus, when we visited my Grandma Beth and Grandpa Joe's on Christmas Day, I asked them how it felt to have homeless people with them for the holiday. They told me they didn't see us as "homeless people" and I shouldn't think of myself that way. "You all are simply going through a rough patch, Davey!" Grandpa Joe said. It felt like more than that to me, but there was no way I could make him understand. They hadn't felt comfortable taking the four of us in when we lost our home. Grandpa Joe came from a family where the motto was *God helps those who help themselves.* So he didn't feel it was right to give us a leg up. He felt my dad needed to find his way back on his own. I thought that was pretty harsh. Maybe that's just me.

6

Fashion Mishaps

In March of 2011, I was still in the fourth grade. That winter had been long and cold. I did not make the Level 2 basketball team. Even so, I didn't complain about it, because I did get to be an official starter that year on the Level 1 team. Not to mention, I was known for having a high assist record and leading my team in scoring! Also, I turned ten, and to celebrate, my friends came over for homemade pizza that Mom had made especially for my big day.

My winter, however, was far from perfect, especially in terms of family. My dad continued to drink, watch a lot of television, and have anger issues that alienated me. He was also becoming rougher with me more often, which I didn't know how to handle. One time he pushed me so hard, I painfully hit the floor and had to sit down for an hour! Another time he threw my basketball at Julia and it just barely missed her! My poor mom was struggling to take care of him as well as Julia and me, and I found her worrying a lot. She knew she needed to ask my dad to leave if he didn't stop terrorizing the family, but she was too afraid. As I mentioned earlier, she had gotten a lot of her self-confidence from Dad, and now she was having trouble finding strength down deep inside of herself. She would often cry and hug me for comfort. Most of her paintings continued to depict very bleak images.

All the tension and stress Mom and Dad were feeling were also beginning to take a toll on Julia. Whenever she asked either of them to play horses with her, Dad yelled at her about how rude it is to interrupt people when they are watching TV. And Mom was usually too busy to play because she was cooking or thinking about important things. Plus, because Julia had a loud voice, when she talked to her stuffed animals or to her doll, Bell, Dad often turned around and yelled, "*Shut up!*" in a way you should *never* do to a first grader, nor to anyone for that matter. But, especially not to a first grader. To protect Julia from Dad's rages, Mom would often have her do sleepovers at Ella's.

As for me, I usually tried to stay out of our toxic, stressful family scene at the inn between dinner and bedtime. I would bundle up, go outside, and either take pictures of the frozen lake nearby, or read the newest book by Mike Lupica that I had from the library. Also, I still had a lot of sleepovers at Justin's.

I was elated with hope when spring rolled around. I imagined the warm weather would improve the mood of everyone in my family. Plus, spring was baseball season which always made me happy. I was equally thrilled when Coach Billy gave me a baseball uniform with the number 5 on it. That was the number Joe DiMaggio had worn! Joe DiMaggio had also been a center fielder, and because of that, he was the baseball player I looked up to the most.

Then, the night of my first baseball game, I went to Max's house for a sleepover.

"Ready for our first game tomorrow, David?" Max asked giving me a high five as I arrived.

I laughed. "It's the other team that should be preparing, Max! We're going to crush'em!"

Max's little brother, Oliver, grinned and nodded. "Watch out, Hedgehogs! Here come the Antelopes!" he punched his fist in the air. Oliver, only a year younger than Max and me, was on the same team as we were.

At that moment, the Clementes' boxer puppy, Jacques, came in. He was still learning his manners at the time and was quite aggressive, but I wasn't afraid of him.

"Hey, boy!" I laughed, lying on the ground and petting him. At that moment, Jacques put his paw on my jersey and gave it a huge scratch, cutting a large hole in the top right part of my jersey.

"Jacques!" scolded Max. "David's nice!" He picked up Jacques and lugged him into the other room. Then, he asked with a look of concern, "You okay?"

"I'm physically fine, I, um, I don't know if I can play in this jersey now!" I groaned as I wondered if I would have to sit out of tomorrow's game because of the tear. "Remind me never to wear a jersey to your house again. Not until your boxer learns to behave!" I said, smiling outwardly even though I was worried, too. I switched shirts and called my mom.

"Can you fix a rip?" I asked her.

"Sure, honey," said Mom. A half hour later, she arrived to pick up my jersey, and the next day, she dropped it at school during lunch.

It was a disaster! Mom had re-stitched the hole in my blue uniform shirt; where the rip had been, Mom had inserted a pink and silver-striped design!

"No! I can't wear this to the game, Mom!" I cried in dismay.

"I'm sorry, David!" she said. "I just didn't have thread in any other color!"

"Mom, I'll be laughed at!"

"No, you won't," Mom reassured me. "You're making too big of a deal of this. Everything will be fine. Trust me."

Again, I was humiliated. I tried wearing the sewn-up jersey. I ended up taking it off when a girl in my class, Lucille Zeno, giggled and said, "That's a cute pink pocket, David!" I grimaced.

"What happened?" asked Alexa. "Were you painting and forgot you're not an easel?"

"Did you want to make a protest on the field?" asked Stacey.

"Nothing you need to know," I told them, walking away.

At game time, I showed Coach Billy. He looked surprised. I told him about Jacques.

"What should I do, Coach?" I asked. He sighed.

"Wear it for this game and tomorrow I'll get you a new jersey."

I hesitated. The different-colored-stitching made me feel divided from the rest of the team; even so, I knew pink-silver thread was better than not getting to play.

"There's nothing wrong with your jersey being a little different, David," Justin told me as we got into the team huddle. "It just means you're unique and awesome while the rest of us are normal and boring."

"Thanks, Justin." I was really lucky to have a best friend like him.

The other team was up first. The first kid up hit the ball out to centerfield and I easily ran over and caught it—*out!* The next kid struck out. The third kid hit it just over the second baseman's head, and, instead of just hitting a single, tried to stretch it into a double. I quickly grabbed the baseball and threw it to Will who was covering second base. Will caught the ball, spun around, and tagged the runner out before he made it to second base. Third out.

We were up.

Robby led off. Unfortunately, he struck out. Oliver was up next. He hit a pitch to left field and glided to first base. Louis batted third and hit the highest pop fly you ever saw. It barely made it out of the infield. The first baseman walked over, looked up into the sky, waited a few seconds, and then it landed smack in his glove. I was up next. As I walked to home plate, the pitcher looked at me and smirked.

"That's quite a fashion statement!" he jeered. "What's that on your jersey, puke?"

Well! If he thought he could get to me with appalling behavior, he was dead wrong! Watch your mouth, pitcher-of-the-other-team, because as the saying goes, *What you say always catches up with you!* I refused to let his behavior bother me or let it prevent me from hitting the ball. Instead, it motivated me! I swung at the first pitch he threw—a huge, angry swing. And when my bat connected, the ball flew and flew, over the fence in left field. *A home run!* 2 - 0.

By the bottom of the fourth inning, we were winning 9 - 3. So, you know what that moron of a pitcher did? When Greg Richardson stepped up to plate, the pitcher aimed it at *him* instead of at the plate and hit him in the thigh! We refused to be intimidated. Instead, our righteous anger for our teammate made us work even harder!

The next time I was up after that pitcher hit Greg was in the bottom of the sixth and I was determined to avenge my team. As I stepped up to bat, I could almost hear the song *Fighter,* by Christina Aguilera, playing in my head, echoing my determination to hit another home run.

By then the score was 11 - 3. The bases were loaded. I thought to myself, *if I hit a home run, they might call the mercy rule and we would win!* So when the ball came, I swung my bat with all my strength and hit the ball over the centerfield fence, not too far from where my earlier hit had ended up.

"Bullies are nothing more than motivation coming to you in a crappy way," I murmured to Justin, who nodded in agreement. Sure enough, after the seventh inning, they called a mercy rule when we were winning 19 - 5! We were over the moon!

"Way to go, guys!" Coach Billy chuckled. "I'm proud of you! You managed to ignore their baiting and rudeness and we won, even with David's torn jersey!"

That's when I had a revelation. Maybe Jacques' scratch had made my jersey *lucky*! The next time I went to Max's house, I gave Jacques a big hug and a pat on the back to say *thank you*.

Little did I know, the jersey event was the first of many clothing incidents that spring to befall my family. The next disaster happened the following weekend. To encourage my father, who had gone from Joe-enthusiastic to being lackadaisical (to put it nicely) about working out, Mom insisted we go on a family bike ride. (Even though we were homeless, Mom made sure we kept our bikes. Some things are just sacred.) Julia and I have both always loved riding bikes, and we were thrilled!

We were riding up a hill when I rang my bicycle bell and shouted at Julia in an obnoxious voice, "Stop thief!"

Julia responded by saying calmly, "You're the robber, since robbers are annoying like you!" and sped off. However, she raced off so quickly I don't think she was paying attention because she ran right into a tree and tore her blue dress! Luckily, she wasn't hurt!

"You, okay?" I asked as she got off her bike.

"Fine, I'll sew it up later," she told me confidently.

Later that night, however, I heard Julia ask, "Mom, do we have any blue thread left?"

"None," Mom replied, checking, just in case. "All we have are these three colors left—green, purple, and pink. Can you use any of those?"

Julia rolled her eyes, then she nodded. When she finished the dress, it looked completely babyish and homemade, and honestly, not very pretty.

"Julia," I told her after she put it on, "you should look in the mirror."

Julia looked, and burst into tears. "My dress is ruined!' she sobbed, "Totally and completely ruined!"

Mom comforted Julia by telling her, "Everything has beauty, Julia, and you know who sees it?" Julia shook her head. "Smart, kind people can see it."

Julia still moaned about her dress for days until Mom made her a new, even prettier, that Julia was overjoyed about—even though it, too, had the same tri-color thread!

There was also Eric O'Malley's middle school graduation. Justin invited me, and Mom wanted to make sure I cleaned up nice that evening. She even got some money from a friend at church to buy me a decent second hand suit at the church flea market!

"Justin and his family have done a lot for us! We have to look good in return!" she told me, tying my necktie on me.

However, I took a quick walk a few minutes later and a teenage boy saw me and threw mud at me for some stupid reason. The suit was ruined!

Mom tried washing it with soap; that just made the mud stain worse.

"Justin is going to be so hurt if I don't show up in a suit," I groaned. "What am I going to do?"

"Ask Justin if you can borrow one of his," Mom suggested.

We rode over to his house. When I nervously asked Justin, he shook his head.

"You look fine, dude," he assured me. "A muddy outfit won't hurt anyone."

The graduation was lots of fun. There was an after-party and we had cake, cookies, and pie. Everyone was focused on the graduation and no one noticed the mud on my suit.

The final clothing-problem incident came on a beautiful July day. Mom and I were taking a walk when a few thugs started jumping in puddles and splashing Mom with mud.

Indignant, I jumped in front of them and shouted, "Stop! What did she ever do to you?"

The thugs laughed and said, "We were just having fun, little boy."

I replied, "You know, we could always call the police. My mother has her phone in her pocket and a little mud won't stop her from taking it out and reporting you guys."

Mom nodded her head to confirm that I was serious, and the thugs nervously looked at each other before running away.

When they were gone, I asked, concerned, "You okay, Mom?"

Mom laughed. "With your uniform, your suit, and Julia's dress," she told me, "I learned a long time ago that ruined clothes are just part of not being where you want to be yet in your life." I just nodded. I completely understood.

A week later, before our final game (my league was together for six months out of the year, through both spring and summer), I went to a movie with Justin, Robby, Louis, and Will.

"Do you want me to pay for you, David?" Will asked.

"Sure, Will, thanks," I said, feeling grateful that, I was no longer secretive with my friends about the fact that I was homeless. In other words, now when friends would make kind offers, I had learned to accept their help. The good news was, we got seats near the front of the theater. The bad news was, some irritating girls from my class were in front of us. Stacey, Alexa, Katie, and Morgan were examining Stacey's ring *very loudly*, and being extremely annoying. Thankfully, they got quiet the moment the movie started. The movie itself was a little boring. It had an antiquated theme from the 1970s about wrestling when they used to make the athletes take steroids causing the average-build guys to get super big and muscle-bound, and to become crazy-addicted to opioids. Fortunately, I was focused on the baseball game we had ahead of us that day.

By the time the boring movie was over, I was restless and ready to play. My friends and I met up with our teammates and we walked onto the field ready to win the championship. Guess what happened? We won! I played the first six innings, made a number of decent catches, and I hit a triple, a single, and a homerun. Will also hit a home run. We ended up winning, 5 - 2.

"I'm proud of you guys. You all worked so hard!" Coach Billy told us, "It makes me really proud to see you guys united. That's how we won. Teamwork!"

After the game I handed my striped jersey to Coach Billy.

"Maybe it will bring another player the good luck it brought me," I told him.

"No, David," Coach Billy said. "Keep it. I want it to remind you how something that seemed terrible turned out to be amazing!" My take-away from that season was not the jersey, but Coach's parting words, "Don't be so quick to be negative. Be positive about the future because we create our fate to a significant extent."

7

A New School

Fifth grade was fast approaching. I was now in middle school and it felt like a whole new world. My friends and I were headed to a new school, where we would be mixing with students from an elementary school on the southeastern side of town.

The middle school was super crowded. To make matters worse, a lot of the girls were wearing ostentatious long dresses to celebrate the beginning of middle school. I can't even begin to tell you how hard it was to navigate around those things—a total tripping hazard! Without them, the school would have felt a lot more navigable. Eric O'Malley also attempted to scare me by trying to trick me into thinking fifth grade teachers screamed at their students.

Nevertheless, I was happy about starting that year. There had been very few clubs at my elementary school. In middle school, however, there were a lot. Justin and I learned that there had once been a tennis club. It had been removed five years earlier. Not enough students at our school had been into tennis at that time. However, Justin and I both enjoyed tennis, so we decided to petition to bring back the club. I was pretty excited and thought I was in for an awesome fifth grade year. That is, until my Science teacher, Miss Chandler, insulted me.

"Study hard through your life, students, or you'll end up idle and aimless, and possibly even homeless!" She actually said that! Then it got even worse. "It has been empirically proven that the majority of homeless people are incompetent and ignorant!"

I was furious. I wanted to punch her, but I restrained myself. How dare she just insult every homeless person in the world without taking into consideration the fact that there might be an actual homeless person in the room! Justin, Nick, Otto, and Eliot were all in my Science class and they shot me sympathetic looks. I buried my emotions behind my scarlet face.

When I told my parents, they spoke to the school principal at once. Although Miss Chandler was neither fired nor forced to apologize, it was satisfying to know she had been lectured by the principal.

In Gym class, I was pleased to hear we were starting off with football. I hadn't played in a long time, even though I enjoyed the game well enough. I also knew that I definitely wouldn't lag behind when we got to indoor basketball.

My Math teacher, Mr. Jordan, was awesome. He taught us a bunch of cool tricks for fractions, such as *Keep Change Flip* (K, C, F). As an unexpected bonus, he told us that if 51% or more of us got a 90 or above on any quiz, he would take us outside to play games the day after that quiz.

Spanish, Art, Social Studies, and English were okay, though a little boring—two really good classes, one awful class, and four half-decent classes. It could have been worse. As for the petition Justin and I had outlined to bring to the tennis club back, we got to work the minute our second week of fifth grade began. We wrote a compelling argument to inspire kids to sign it.

"Tennis is good for your health, a great way to get to know people, and a fun sport overall! Sign this if you want a fun, new way to be healthier, and to get to make new friends!"

We only needed seventy signatures, and we got a lot right away, including a tall, blond, show-offy eighth grade boy nicknamed Swag.

"I'd be happy to join," crooned Swag, swaggering up and grabbing my pen. "I'll use my strong ambidextrous hands to hit the ball all the way to China!"

After we showed the principal our petition, she said she would talk it over with the School Board. We wondered if she was being evasive, but we knew better than to talk back. As it turned out, we got approval, and the tennis club came back, with a lot of excited members—including Swag.

Meanwhile, at the inn, things were looking alright— well, as alright as things could possibly be when you're indigent. Dad was still going to bars and drinking a lot to numb the pain of his blighted reputation and financial failure. He continued to be a difficult person to live with, although he *did* decide to *resume* his Alcoholics Anonymous meetings.

Julia was in second grade and had become very good at Spanish. In fact, she constantly spoke it at the dinner table just to show off. Mom was still trying to handle our tough situation as well as she could without losing her marbles. I could tell by her paintings that she had been feeling more hopeful lately, because the images were a bit more upbeat. Her recent paintings included our whole family biking on a sunny day, a picture of her and Dad kissing, me playing baseball with some friends, and

Julia horseback riding. On the bike painting, she wrote six words: *"Good times are on the way."* That was something my whole family needed to believe for sure! Mom also spent time with her friends from our church and with Julia's and my friends' parents. They supported her mood and gave her a lot of comfort.

At school, our new tennis club was a lot of fun, too. Twenty-five super energized students showed up to play at the gym every Wednesday after school. I was pretty good at tennis, possibly because my baseball skills helped me do well swinging the racket, hitting the ball, and scoring a fair amount of points. We worked in pairs and I usually paired up with Justin or Robby or Will who were also fairly passionate tennis players. And our team usually won. However, kids beat us a bunch of times, too.

"We beat you, *Hobbit!*" a super tall eighth grade girl shouted as she hit the ball out of the tennis court. Oh, how I absolutely loathed just how many people called me by my most-hated nickname when they beat me in a set.

"You're just prejudiced against short people," I snarled.

Justin stood up for me. "David isn't that short!"

"Just vertically challenged," a girl shot back.

"Hey, you wouldn't even be playing here if it weren't for David!" Justin yelled.

After that, they were quiet about *Hobbit*, and got back to the business of playing tennis.

All in all, middle school was actually going pretty well. That is, until one of the lunch ladies crossed a line and crushed Julia's self-esteem. It was October and Nick, Louis, and I went to a high school football game. Aside from the fact that two nerds in front of us in the bleachers were discussing the composition of a football super loudly, it was fun. Even though we were losing by a lot—something that seemed to have stressed a number of the football players—every touchdown completely thrilled my friends and me. When it was over, we climbed down the bleachers to the sidelines and found our ride home.

Nick's Aunt Elisa, who worked as a lunch lady at our school, had agreed to drive us home. Louis's sister, Shanice, and Nick's sister, Sienna, were both good friends with Julia, and they were actually at the inn along with a bunch of Julia's other friends that afternoon. Nick's Aunt the lunch lady planned to pick up Shanice and Sienna when she dropped me off. My stop was first since I lived the closest to the school. When we arrived at the inn, Ms. Elisa's jaw dropped.

"*You-you're* homeless, David?"

"Um, yeah," I said quietly as I quickly opened the car door to get out.

"Do your parents—?"

"I don't have time to answer these questions," I snapped, feeling very uncomfortable as I walked quickly away from the car.

"Hey, honey, how was the game?" Mom hollered from the front porch of our inn room.

"Good, though unfortunately, I think we're still—"

"Mrs. Kimball! Hi, I'm Nick's aunt; could I ask you a few questions?"

I whirled around in surprise, suddenly realizing that Ms. Elisa had followed Mom and me into our inn room! I scowled and put my hands on my hips.

"Why don't you go be nosey somewhere else?" I muttered and took Mom's hand, dragging her toward our room to escape the intrusive woman.

"David, be nice," Mom scolded, before saying politely as she opened the door to our room, "Yes, Elisa, what's up?"

"What on earth happened that caused you guys to lose your house?"

The woman really creeped me out. Why the heck was it any of her business!? Not to mention the fact that she was asking this right when Julia had eight friends over! In fact, I could see Julia in her corner of the room looking confused and upset. Thankfully, I could see Julia's friends were reassuring her that everything would be okay and to ignore Ms. Nosey-body.

We suffered through ten long minutes of Ms. Elisa's interrogation. Finally, my mom was so uncomfortable she responded politely to her questions. That's when I made what I would much later learn was called an executive decision. I decided to get Ms. Elisa to leave. Thank God Dad was out—even if he *was* at a bar.

"My dad is coming home later if you want to come back and interview *him*," I blurted out, opening the door and gesturing for her to step out. Ms. Elisa looked a bit flustered. Thankfully, she took the hint and left.

Mom quickly led Sienna and Shanice outside to join Sienna's aunt and their brothers, and once Mom was back in our room, she shook her head.

"Well, that was atrocious," Mom scoffed.

Later that evening, after all Julia's friends had left, my little sister, close to tears, asked, "Mom, wh-what did that woman mean when she kept calling us homeless?"

I went outside to the porch and read *Summer Ball*, because I did not want to hear Mom explain the horrible truth. Periodically, I looked up from my book to peer through the window as Mom explained to Julia that we were homeless. It broke my heart again to see Julia's self-esteem fall into the gutter as she sobbed and sobbed! Ugh, it was awful!

"Let's get our lunch in *that* line, Justin," I said the next day as Justin and I headed into the lunchroom the next day.

Justin frowned. "Why, David? The one we usually take is less crowded."

The reason I didn't want our normal line was because I didn't want to face Nick's annoying aunt who was a server in our line.

"Nick's aunt completely disrespected my family and broke Julia's heart last night," I burst out, then Justin the whole story.

"That woman is always rude and nosy, David," said Justin. "Once, when Nick was over and Ms. Elisa and Mrs. Lance came to pick him up, my mom came out wearing a super pretty dress and Nick's aunt asked her how much it cost, and how often she bought new party dresses in the past month!"

"Maybe she's just stupid?" I wondered out loud.

Then I went into the crowded line and Justin, always loyal as a knight showing fealty to his king, went with me. I was super grateful to him for that since, yes, a shorter line, and therefore, a longer amount of time to eat lunch, is definitely preferable to the long wait at the crowded line! We ate lunch and talked about sports until it was time for class.

In Language Arts that afternoon, we had to write an essay about an idea we had and why it was a good one. I wrote about how Nick's aunt should take a manners class. As usual, after writing about how mad I was, I felt a lot better. Keeping a journal has always helped me feel better. I think everyone should try it.

Yet even as I headed to Gym class through the barely navigable halls, with Justin and Max breaking a path for me through the crowd of students, I couldn't *un-remember* the pain of Nick's aunt mistreating my family. Even worse, when anyone talked to Julia now back at the inn, our homelessness became the focus of every single conversation! By the end of the week, Mom and I were tired from the endless conversations in which Julia would ask, "Why are we homeless? What did we do to deserve it?"

Mom tried to explain that our family was equally special no matter where we lived. Julia was too smart for that. Even when mom pointed out that most horses don't have homes—since Julia takes pride in everything she has in common with horses—did not work. A week later, Julia went to Ella's for a sleepover, giving Mom and me some time to discuss how to make her feel better about not having a real home.

"We need to keep Julia's self-image from being completely annihilated," Mom said that evening, "We need her to remember that she is a sweet, funny, smart, beautiful girl with deep commitments to her family and friends."

"Not to mention a deep commitment to being a *clothes horse*. I mean she loves clothes and horses," I added, and Mom and I giggled for the first time in a very long time. "But, Mom, how *do* we fix this for her?"

Suddenly, my father barged in. He was clearly drunk and slurred his words as he shouted, "We need to have an intervention on how much you use your cell phone, Charlotte! Do you want to pay extra this month?"

Intervention! That was it! I saw a look in my mother's eyes that I had not seen for a long time—it was *hope.*

"David!" she whispered calmly to me after Dad tried to make her feel crazy, "I have an idea! Let's give both Julia and Dad interventions. Julia's this Saturday, Dad's the next."

With no mind to Dad's presence, which Mom ignored blatantly because she knew when he was drunk and he didn't listen to anything anyway, she explained *intervention* to me. "An intervention is when a group of loving, caring friends and family get together to contradict someone's negative belief about themselves, to help them break through denial about negative behaviors, such as addictions or other forms of self-abuse, or to address some other kind of mistake they were making."

I agreed that an intervention would be the perfect thing to rehabilitate Julia's self-esteem. As for my dad, well, we'd get to him in due course.

That Saturday, a few of Julia's teachers and a bunch of her friends came over. At first, Julia wasn't happy about this because she was missing her riding lesson at the free program. She even asked if she didn't deserve to ride horses because she was homeless. Instead of answering her question directly, we all took turns talking about how sweet, smart, and funny Julia was, how good she was at the things she loved, and how much fun we had being with her.

Then Mom said, "You see? The fact that we do not *own* our own home does not cancel out your *awesomeness*, Julia!"

That was when Julia began to nod and cry.

"Thank you," she whispered.

I gave my little sister a hug. We'd done it! We'd given her enough affirmation to gain back her self-esteem! Mission accomplished!

In English class, we were now going over poems with good cadence. Justin was in my class, so we wrote one together. It was about a boy who was trying to stop being a bully.

"Maybe this poem can be used to advocate for anti-bullying," Justin suggested.

"Yeah," I agreed, "That's very important. I don't understand why bullies do what they do. Do the people they hurt have no value to them?"

Justin nodded and shrugged. He wasn't exactly sure either.

"When I was five, I was kind of overweight," Justin told me, "A boy used me as his toy punching bag, saying all my flab would prevent my stomach from hurting when he punched it. He could not have been more wrong! It hurt like crazy when he punched me." Justin told me all about the jerk who had bullied him and all the pain the boy had caused. Then, Justin chuckled, got up, and flexed his arms. He lifted his shirt a little so I could see his developing six-pack. Then Justin added,

"Wish he could see me now! Thanks for the inspiration, dung-head!"

I nodded. "Justin, if you and that idiot ever were to meet again face-to-face, you could probably beat him up easily!" I suggested, before confiding to Justin, "When I was four, I made all these super weird and inappropriate comments, asking creepy questions like 'how's your stomach?' and 'how well do you know your mom?' which caused me to struggle to make friends. My nickname was *Mr. Weirdo.*"

"You've come a long way, Dave." Justin grinned. "I can't possibly picture you being such a creep. Though to be honest, you still had a little of the weirdness in first grade. I remember it." Winking he added, "It's okay, Dave. You're fine now." We laughed.

(Our bully poem turned out pretty well. It was a graded assignment in English, and Justin and I got a 96.5% on it.)

I felt like I was becoming more mature. I was only ten, soon to be eleven. However, I felt like I was becoming more grown-up. The past couple of years, I'd only discussed things like sports, my friends, homelessness, video games, and movies. However, these days, I was talking with my mom and my friends about issues like politics, crime, and other events in the news. Fifth grade had definitely changed me quite a bit. It made me feel smarter and more mature.

Mom and I also talked more about giving Dad an intervention. Although he no longer hung out with brutes like the guys he'd brought to the inn almost a year earlier, he was only attending AA meetings sporadically and was still drinking heavily, as well as living a life that didn't include much discipline. So, a week after Julia's intervention, we invited some dads of my friends and Julia's friends, plus the husbands of some of the members of Mom's church ladies' club, and even a few old work buddies who were not as hard on Dad as the rest of Wood Creek. We also hosted some recovering alcoholics at the inn who understood what Dad was going through and wanted to help, as well as an addictions counselor who worked with homeless addicts and alcoholics and helped them find treatment. They all came over and helped us talk to Dad about changing his lifestyle and reminded him how much potential he really had—if he would just stop drinking, take care of himself, and put his life back together.

However, Dad just snorted and said, "I'm done working. I can't work anywhere without everyone boycotting the place, and I need my escape!" He also said that he didn't *deserve* the right to work after what had happened to the little girl who was kidnapped on his watch. After all of the people left our room, Dad's embarrassment at having been confronted resulted in him gas-lighting Mom again by making it seem like she was to blame, that *she* was the one needing the intervention. Dad's intervention was clearly not nearly as successful as Julia's, although the addictions counselor left me an Alateen card and told me I could call him any time for support.

Mom and I realized that if Dad was going to pull back on his alcoholism and get his life together, something extreme was going to have to happen. The only question was what? We were already living in extreme conditions.

8

Bully Problems

In third and fourth grade, I hadn't faced that much bullying despite the fact that I was homeless. In third grade that made sense because Justin was the only one who actually knew I was homeless. In fifth grade, however, after middle school began, kids seemed to become more judgmental. Apparently, when my peers reached middle school age, their parents had over-shared to them about my dad. The next thing I knew, kids were calling me *hobo* and *tramp*, spreading rumors about me, and punching me with the genius justification that they were trying to prove they weren't afraid of my alcoholic father coming to beat them up. And let me just say, as a ten-year-old, it was extremely frightening.

Part of the scariness in this was that I had no idea which blabbermouths were the ringleaders. I knew that not every student was evil enough to spread those nasty rumors. I wanted to get some idea of who they were, though, to find a way to gain solid information so that I could report them to the school principal. Maybe she could talk to them about being kind to everyone, no matter what they lived in.

I was experiencing so much mental instability from all of this that the school got me a tutor because my grades plummeted. My parents almost refused to let me play basketball that winter! I was being beaten up constantly. By Halloween, I couldn't even eat lunch because my stomach was in so much pain from getting punched in the gut every day. I could hardly eat breakfast or dinner either. As a result, my already skinny body became gaunt: I was almost a stick figure!

"Dude, you really need to eat more," Justin chastised me as we walked to lunch the day after Halloween. "Also, why did you only eat five of the candies you got yesterday when we went trick-or-treating? If you lose more weight, you'll end up in the hospital!"

"You know how I've been bullied so much lately for being homeless?" I told Justin. "Well here is the legacy of all of it." I removed my shirt and showed him my stomach, which was horribly bruised and looked like something from a Gothic horror movie. Justin gasped in shock.

"Have you even gone to the nurse, David? Or filed a complaint with the principal?"

I winced. "I'm too afraid, Justin," I sighed. "What power do they really have to stop it—or prevent the bullies from making my beatings worse for being a tattletale?" I saw that look in Justin's eyes and I caved. "Okay, yes, the nurse does sound like a good idea."

Through gritted teeth, Justin said, "Just because you're homeless—that really isn't right!" Justin's dark eyes flashed angrily before he threw a comforting arm around my shoulder and walked me to the nurse.

When we entered the nurse's office, I showed her my stomach. Her blue eyes bulged out of her head. "*Wha— what* happened?" she stammered.

Justin told her how I was being used as a punching bag several times a day because I was homeless. The nurse looked shocked and angry. She examined my stomach and every cut and bruise. She washed the cuts with a cloth that smelled unpleasant like alcohol. Then she said that I needed to name my attackers. The nurse also suggested I eat my lunch in her office for a while, at least until my stomach was healed enough to be comfortable eating lunch again. And she took photographs of my stomach and filed them in her computer. After that, she called my mom, and presumably also the principal. Although I didn't know it at the time, she called in a social worker who was able to single out the bullies and meet up with them individually. They would talk about how bullying was wrong. Eventually, after the social worker had met with all of the bullies, he had a meeting with them, the principal, and their parents, and they were all suspended for a blissful week and a half.

That first day, when I got home from school, my mom was in tears.

"Oh, baby!" she wailed as she threw her arms around me. "I had no idea you're being bullied!" She hugged me gently and led me inside where she gave me homemade cookies.

"Justin's mom gave me the ingredients and allowed me to make them at her house," she explained. She paused before asking, "Do you want to be homeschooled for a little while? At least until all of your injuries heal?"

I shook my head firmly. "No, Mom, the bullies aren't chasing me away like a scared little puppy," I told her firmly. "Too much has been taken from our family. I'm not letting my education be taken away too." My mother began to tear up again.

"That's my brave baby. *Please* make sure that you find a way to protect yourself before things get worse! Otherwise, mark my words, I will pull you out of school, *and* I will sue that God-forsaken school and the families of every bully in that place!"

Justin was several steps ahead of my mom. That night, he called and asked if I could come over for an emergency meeting. Mom let me go, even though it was on the late side. When I got to Justin's house, our whole friend group was in the O'Malley living room. Otto and Nick were sitting on the floor. Eliot, Max, and Robby were on one couch, while Louis, Sam, and Will sat attentively on the other. Justin was poised to hold court in a wing-back chair. Beside him was a second chair. He gestured for me to sit.

"Okay, guys," said Justin.

Robby was the first to stand.

"David, Justin told us about what you have been going through," said Robby with his hands on his hips. "It ends right now!"

"Robby's right," Otto added. "We've got a plan for your protection. Never use the bathroom during class time again. Instead, wait until the end of class and tell one of us you need to go. At least one of us will walk with you to the boy's room and guard your stall, if necessary."

"We are also walking you from class to class," Nick chimed in. "We've always walked from class to class together, especially if we have two classes in a row together. Now we are going to make sure we *always* do—and that you are never on the edge of the group."

"We're helping too, Dave," Sam told me. "Me and Louis and Will, the sixth graders. Our period one English class is in the same hall as your period one Spanish class. And then we have Math period-two, just like you—in the same hallway! Since Eliot is the only one of us in both your Spanish and Math classes, we figured you'd need additional bodyguards during that walk—especially on days, God forbid, that Eliot can't make it to school."

"We're also going to go with you to the nurse's office and walk you to period-five afterwards," Justin informed me, "All nine of us will eat with you to keep you company and we'll fend off any bullies no matter what."

"I also called Pete and told him what's going on and if the bullying gets worse, he's flying back from Miami to beat those bullies senseless," Louis concluded. (Our friend Pete Zimmerman had moved to Florida over the summer.)

Max walked over and put an arm around me.

"You aren't alone, David. We will protect you by any means necessary!" he told me firmly.

"Yeah, we've totally got your back, man," said Eliot.

I could feel myself sniffling. The ten of us (eleven of us when Peter lived in Wood Creek) had all been friends since first and second grade; this, however, was the first time we had formed a bodyguard system. I was very grateful and couldn't stop myself from going around and giving them all bro-hugs.

"Thanks a million, guys!" I said gratefully. "I—I don't know how to say it better than that."

"You don't have to, Dave," said Eliot.

"You'd do the same if it was any of us," added Will.

The bodyguard system was definitely helpful. The social worker's behind-the-scenes interventions were helpful as well. The bullying decreased a lot over the next couple of weeks and then the bullies all got an "extended vacation" the week and a half before Thanksgiving vacation. Plus, when they got back (under the social worker's watchful eye, probably) they stopped the physical abuse, and one guy even apologized. However, many of them turned to verbal bullying. While the insults were easier to ignore, sometimes the rude words got to me. Also, terrible rumors about me were still flying all over the school. On the upside, I was really developing a thick skin and learning to advocate for myself.

One day, shortly after Thanksgiving, I was in Gym class hanging out with Justin, Nick, Max, and Robby. The five of us had just finished playing *Knock-out* and were trying to decide what to play next when a pair of kids from one of the most popular groups in the fifth grade approached us. I knew that their names were Andrew and Connor. And I didn't trust either of them. Since September, I had noticed that both of them were arrogant and mean, as well as good at sports—good at almost everything, in fact, except kindness. Their families were also extremely rich, and they were always wearing the fanciest of everything! Both of them had played a major part in the transformation of my stomach into a Gothic work of art. (By now my stomach had started healing a little, even though most of the grotesque bruising was still visible.)

"Are you going to your daddy's trial, Davy?" one of them sneered.

"First of all, please don't call me *Davy*. I don't even let my friends call me that," I told them calmly. "And second of all, I don't know what the heck you're talking about. What trial?"

"Our parents went to a bar last weekend and overheard your dad talking about how he hit Julia, whoever that is. They were suspicious and wanted to get more information. So they followed your dad out of the bar and saw him vandalize a church with swear words!

They waited till this morning they called the police. They wanted to make sure you were at school, to prevent you from having to witness your dad's big humiliation. Then the cops arrested him."

What? I could not believe it. It was impossible because I had been at home with my parents the whole time. And Dad spray paint a church? That was an absolute lie! My dad would never do something that would be so harmful to Mom, who loved the Church! Dad was drunk and violent at times, but he would never, *ever* hurt Mom so deeply.

I wanted to call those evil boys liars, thugs, and a bunch of other horrible names, but I was scared that *that* would just result in more beatings, even with my bodyguard-buddies right there at my side. So instead, I backed away.

I tried not to think about Andrew and Connor and their claims. *That* lasted about a minute. As soon as Gym class let out and Justin and I were walking home, I broke down in tears.

"What if those guys' parents really called the police? And even though there was absolutely no proof—could the police have arrested my dad without any evidence?" I whimpered.

"I doubt it," Justin replied, comfortingly. "You shouldn't listen to them, David!"

However, I was still very afraid. We reached the inn and said goodbye. I went inside to confirm my fears. And there was Dad, slouched on the sofa, drinking beer and watching television as usual! I almost cried out in relief.

"Yes!" I squealed.

"What, honey?" Mom asked, looking up from her painting.

"Dad's not in jail!" I rejoiced, and told Mom what the boys had said.

She was furious! "That's unacceptable!" she shrieked. "I'm going to report this! Harry, do you want to come?"

Dad turned around. "Huh?" *That's progress,* I thought. *At least he's responding now.* Mom told him what happened, and he nodded. "I'm coming for sure," he said firmly.

The next day, my parents went straight to the school to report those wicked boys.

I was in Math class when the announcement came over the PA system, "David Kimball, please report to the main office." I knew what this was about, and I could not wait to testify against Andrew and Connor who were already in the office with their parents by the time I got there. The parents were sitting and staring stone-faced at my dad, like he was the Joker or Lex Luther or some other comic book villain. *Dad's not a villain! Stop looking at him like he is,* I thought bitterly as I watched them closely before the principal held court.

"David, is it true that these two gentlemen claimed your father was in jail?" Principal Trenton asked. She was a kind young woman who was known to be intelligent and fair-minded.

"Yes," I said at once.

"Andrew? Connor?"

"It was a joke! Can't David take a joke?" Andrew sneered.

"Yeah! It's not our fault David is ridiculously sensitive and can't even handle a little teasing!" Connor added.

Everyone knew about my bruised stomach already, of course; even so, I didn't think it was a bad idea to show everyone again. I lifted my shirt. The bruises were still greenish-yellow, though I had healed somewhat. Their parents gasped.

"I've faced loads of bullying because my family is homeless," I said plainly. "It's hard to not feel sensitive. Especially after you look at this disgusting masterpiece which several other kids, including Connor and Andrew, have created by hitting and kicking me!"

"We already got suspended for that!" Andrew exclaimed. "And we haven't touched you all week! Don't try to get us punished even more, David! Get over it!"

"Plus, you can't be tried twice for the same crime," added Connor.

His lawyer-father immediately shushed him and whispered something in his ear. Connor shut up.

Wow, I thought in disgust. How in the world was I supposed to get over the physical part of the bullying when the verbal part, which was almost as bad, was still a part of my life?!

"Yeah, David. You are probably just jealous of how awesome we are." Connor added. He turned to my dad and said jeeringly, "Now, Mr. Kimball, don't beat *us* up for saying that!" Again, Connor's father put his hand on Connor's arm and glowered at his son.

Dad went bright red. I was enraged! How dare he insult my father like that! Worse, his parents didn't call him out for being rude! I was *furious* at them for that!

"Connor Manchel! Apologize!" exclaimed Principal Trenton.

"We don't apologize to homeless losers, especially not sensitive *girls*, or violent morons," Andrew retorted hotly.

"I'm warning you..."

"Even if we do apologize, it won't change the fact these people are pathetic," said Connor.

"It has changed one fact, Connor," Principal Trenton replied. "The two of you are expelled from this school, effective immediately!"

"*Wha*—expelled? You can't do that!" Mrs. Manchel replied.

"She's right," agreed Andrew's dad. "Our boys were just having a little fun. Can't David take a joke?"

"It was *not* funny. It was hurtful, insensitive, inappropriate slander," replied the principal. She stood up and because she was awfully tall, she seemed intimidating. "Now please leave this school and do *not* bother to reapply next year."

The two bullies hung their heads and left the school—with their furious parents, who muttered curse words as the six of them departed.

I felt happier than I had in weeks! "Thank you, Mrs. Trenton," I said gratefully, as the bullies were escorted out to the exit door by the assistant principal.

"David, listen. If anyone else gives you trouble, you just let me know!"

Wow, she was nice.

Almost overnight, the rumors and insults vanished into the air! No one dared to say anything mean to me again. I can't even begin to say just how relieved I was when the bullying completely stopped, and my life started to feel more normal.

As basketball season approached, I spent as much time as possible practicing in the school gym. Sam gave me an old hoop he found which I brought to the inn to practice my shots. My parents even agreed to buy new gym clothes to practice in, as mine no longer fit. I had grown a little taller (though I was still quite short), and my body was being savaged by hormonal changes. Both things—the new clothes and the extra height—made life easier. Luxuries like a basketball hoop and new clothes made it seem like I was progressing away from poverty— just a little.

I also made it to the next level team in my basketball league that year. That was really exciting. Especially since Louis was already on it and Sam, Max, and Nick also made it. Tryouts were the last three days of November, and I got the good news on December 7th. I was sick that day, though not contagious, so I had tagged along with my mom, who was having tea at the home of one of her friends from church, a friendly older woman named Judy.

"How's basketball going?" Judy asked me. That was when I remembered about the tryouts.

"Mom, can we check if I made the freshman team?" My mother nodded and logged onto WoodCreekOhioCommunityBasketball.com through her cell phone and checked the Level Two Tryout page. Right above Lance, it said, *David Kimball. Yes! Yes!! YES!!!*

"I made it!"

Mom gave me a hug. "You have faced a lot of challenges this past year!" she praised me. "From dealing with all the clothing issues this spring, to helping Julia with her insecurities when she found out the inn was not a real home, to dealing with all the bullying, to making the basketball team. I am very proud of you for ending your 2011 with as many triumphs as you have!"

"Your whole family has overcome a lot," Judy added kindly. "From what you tell me, Charlotte, Harrison is finally working on his alcohol problem. David has come through so much. Julia survived learning the truth about her 'home' and is still an extraordinary *equestrienne*, athlete, and stylist. And *you*, Charlotte, are an amazing mother and wife—*and artist*—who has done a great job keeping her family together!"

"Thank you!" Mom beamed.

Little did we know that 2012 would bring my family's biggest challenge of all.

9

Julia in Trouble

At last it was Christmas. I was surprised—and pleased—that the adults at the inn actually helped each other a lot during the holidays. At this point, my parents had made a community of friends at the inn, including the Watsons, the elderly couple I had first met at my yard sale. For the holidays, these new friends all made each other presents.

Our family spent Christmas dinner with the O'Malleys, and I gave Justin a really nice bat. He seemed uncomfortable with the gift, especially since my family needed the money for much more important things like food.

"How can you afford to buy me such a great quality bat when you can't afford a house?" Justin asked me incredulously.

I laughed before explaining, "I actually found it in the junk pile that I sold stuff from last year. It used to belong to Mr. Watson, another resident from the inn who is actually friends with my parents, and he was fine giving it to me to give to you."

After Christmas dinner, when Justin and I were playing video games, we overheard my parents telling Mr. and Mrs. O'Malley about life at the inn during the holidays. Mom mentioned how much the gifts they had exchanged had meant particularly to the single and mentally ill people at the inn—a huge percentage of whom were utterly alone.

My mom then said something that made me realize how much the community at the inn had not only helped the lonely people at the inn, but also how they had helped my dad. She told the O'Malleys, "One of the residents at the inn pointed me to a clinic that has helped Harry tremendously. They work with alcoholics who are also homeless."

"It's been really helpful. I haven't had a drink in two weeks, which is a record for me," Dad added humbly. "I know that having a sponsor and going to the AA meetings is making all the difference." I felt a huge surge of gratitude for whoever had told my mom about the clinic. I suddenly realized that Dad had been significantly calmer lately. And I appreciated the people at the inn more. I began to understand that we were all in this together.

After the holidays, the first few weeks of January were great. I enjoyed being on the Level 2 basketball team in my league and having four of my buddies with me. I didn't get a lot of playing time because I was playing on a bigger team than I was used to. However, I did get a few minutes every game and I made the most of those minutes. School was also going pretty well. I'd never been passionate enough about school to be a straight-A student, but my grades were definitely improving. I even had an A-minus in Spanish!

I also turned eleven and my parents gave me the best surprise party ever. They were able to get my basketball coach, Coach Elijah, to host the party in the indoor gym at his beautiful home. I had fun both with my regular group of friends and my new friends from the team, all playing basketball together. After we finished our game, we ate a delicious apple pie made by my dad who seemed to be doing better! (In the Kimball household, we always got apple pie for our birthdays instead of cake.) It was awesome.

Then came Friday, January 20th. It was a completely ordinary day—or at least I thought it was. I was in Math class, and we were supposedly working on *IXL*, a website that gave math and English questions. Nick, Elliot, and I had fooled the teacher into thinking we were on *IXL*, even though we were secretly playing computer games on our laptops without Mr. Jordan having the least bit of suspicion. It was a good thing he didn't do constant sweep checks. However, as I laughed and hung out with my friends, our match being close to victory, something dreadful was transpiring. As the bell rang, the secretary came in and talked to Mr. Jordan quietly. In turn, he gestured for me to approach his desk.

"David, please stay here for a minute."

After the other students cleared out of the classroom, both teachers looked at me, seemingly afraid to speak to me directly.

"David, your father is in the office," the secretary said.

I nodded nervously. As we walked through the halls, my sense of dread increased with each step closer to the principal's office. Maybe this was another awful joke?

When I entered the office, my dad was sitting there looking very grave. His eyes were red and I could tell that he had been crying.

"David, I borrowed a car from Mr. O'Malley. We're going to the hospital right now."

"Why, Dad?" I asked in confusion.

"I'll explain in the car," Dad replied in a firm, gentle voice.

We got into Justin's dad's fancy blue car. Before Dad started to drive, he hit the steering wheel angrily. "Julia fainted in school!" he began, before choking on a sob. He breathed heavily before continuing in a hushed voice, "David, she fell on the stairs and is currently unconscious."

"Seriously? Unconscious from *what*?" *From fainting or from hitting her head?* I wondered. I couldn't believe it. I didn't want to believe it! How can anyone accept the fact that their sibling is unconscious? Dad drove so fast, I was afraid to press him with any more questions. I wondered if he was breaking the speed limit.

When we finally got to the hospital, Dad put his arm around me and led me to the waiting room. Normally I would have looked at sports magazines; right now, though, I was way too worried. My mom was there already, sitting by herself and crying softly with her eyes cast down. She looked up when Dad gave her a gentle tap on the shoulder.

"Charlotte, I got David," whispered my dad.

Mom looked at me. "Oh, baby!" I hugged her tightly.

"Where's Julia?" I asked.

"Doctors are settling her in her hospital room, prepping her for surgery," Mom said, looking me right in the eye, trying to gauge how I was doing with what was happening. "She has to have brain surgery before we can visit her, sweetie." I sat in the seat next to my mother waiting for her to explain more. Dad sat on her other side with his arm around her. The three of us just sat there, quietly and somberly.

"How'll we afford Julia's treatment?" I asked curiously. Mom explained how we had to go in as indigents—we would get Julia her proper care now and, Mom hoped, find some way to pay later. She thought something called Medicare would probably be able to help us, but she wasn't sure. Feeling utterly overwhelmed and scared, I did a little more crying, before reclining on my mother's lap and taking a nap.

A few hours later, I awoke to someone ruffling my hair—Dad. Something smelled like chicken nuggets. My stomach grumbled. "I got you some food, Dave." I opened my eyes as Dad placed boxed fried chicken on my lap along with a salad. I was grateful and I thanked him.

"Is Julia still...?" I probed for information, and glanced at the big clock at the center of the waiting room.

"I'm afraid so, honey," Dad replied. However, shortly after I finished eating, a nurse came into the waiting room. She was petite like my mom, with gray hair and blue eyes.

"Julia is in post-op. I'll take you to see her right now."

"Thank you, ma'am," Mom replied graciously as we followed the nurse to Julia's room.

When we got there, I could not have been less prepared for what I saw: Julia's face was slightly red and had absolutely no expression. Her entire head was bandaged in white like a turban, or a mummy. Because I was in shock, that's where my mind went. There were needles connecting her arm to a bag of dark red blood and a bag of clear saline. I could barely hear her breath as she slept. There was also a dreadful bump on her forehead, which I realized sadly was where she had hit the floor after fainting. It was all too much for me.

Hot tears trickled from my eyes. Everything had been taken away from me and my family! Everything! First my dad's job, then the possessions I'd always taken for granted, then our house, then even our car! Dad nearly lost himself to alcohol addiction, which he was still struggling with, and now my seven-year-old sister could be facing an early death. It was too much. I was angry. I had had enough of enduring this catastrophic, poverty-ridden life! My dad gazed sadly at Julia, breathing heavily. Mom was on her knees beside Julia's bed. She wept and prayed quietly.

"How pretty she is," Mom whispered, sniffling.

"She's a little angel!" the nurse agreed.

I, however, did not find the sight pretty at all. The bag of blood going into Julia's arms terrified me. The nurse regarded us, probably assessing whether my family had adjusted sufficiently to the initial shock of the alarming sight of Julia's state. After a couple of minutes, another woman, who was thin with glasses and blond hair and wore a white coat, entered the room. I guessed she was the doctor. The two women whispered to each other before this new person addressed my parents.

"It's good to see you, Mr. and Mrs. Kimball. My name is Dr. Gordon. I am Julia's surgeon. If this is a convenient time, I would like to discuss her condition with you."

I held my breath watching her mouth move—it was like a surreal slow-motion film. Part of me hoped the doctor would talk in language that was too sophisticated for a fifth grader to understand—no luck there either. I understood every word.

"How much had Julia been eating before she fainted?" Dr. Gordon asked.

"Not much," Mom replied anxiously. "My husband, my son, Julia, and I have gotten accustomed to having a lot less food than we used to. Sometimes, my husband or I have to skip a meal, or one of us has to have just an apple or a granola bar as our dinner. Three meals a day with the three different food groups is extremely rare for us these days. I try to give my kids as much food as possible. It's been a challenge, though, because of our financial situation."

Dr. Gordon frowned, and glanced at the heart and blood pressure monitors next to Julia's bed. She also took a moment to inspect the IV's sticking out of Julia's left arm. It made me even more queasy to look at them.

"Okay. Well, the most important thing for you to know is that the surgery was a success. Unfortunately, Julia is nevertheless still not out of the woods yet. My understanding is that Julia fainted as a result of a lack of nutrition that caused muscle fatigue. Her fall resulted in a brain bleed, or subdural hematoma. During surgery, we evacuated the blood, which was critical in order to decrease the shifting of the brain that might have occurred from the bleed. It's called a *craniotomy*.

"Currently, many of Julia's muscles do not have the food they need to have the energy to function. As a result, they are struggling to work. So we have her on a feeding tube to make sure she gets the nutrients she needs to get strong again. Still, she is currently in a coma and I'm sorry, her prognosis is unclear. I know this will be hard for you to hear. Based on similar cases, it is unclear whether she will wake up or not. And even if she does, she will probably not be able to take part in extracurricular activities or even go to school for a long time. She will need physical therapy to remind all her body parts how to work together again and do their jobs, including her brain. There is hope!"

I could not believe what I was hearing! My sister only *might* wake up? No one, certainly not an eleven-year-old, can fully process the idea of a family member facing an early death or remaining in a coma like a vegetable. The doctor's words sounded garbled to me as she told Mom how they had attached bags of blood and saline to Julia to help restore her. She said that each bag contains sugar, protein, and other nutrients that normal people get from food.

But I could not bear to pay attention. I was in shock, fury, and grief. Once again, I reflected on all the terrible things that had happened over the past two and a half years. Why couldn't Dad have been more careful when he hired that drug dealer? It was crystal clear that his job-loss was the cause of poor Julia's failing health, as well as the many other awful things that had happened to our family.

To comfort themselves, and to pass the time, Mom and Dad spent the afternoon looking at scrapbooks Dad brought to the hospital from the inn. There were pictures from when Julia was a baby, pictures of Julia from when she was a four-year-old *equestrienne*, and a book with pictures of both of us with our friends throughout the years.

Occasionally Mom or Dad would make a comment like, "Bet Nina and Genevieve wish Julia was with them riding the triple saddle pony right now," or "She was so happy after that first dive she took at our old lake house."

At 3:30 p.m., I was tearfully overseeing Julia in her bed and watching for any signs of motion while she slept. Suddenly I heard the door open and looked up in surprise. Twelve girls bustled into the room carrying cards and wildflowers. The majority of them looked older than Julia—other than Shanice Allen, who was her age. Several of them were crying as they placed their flowers and cards on Julia's bed. One girl, whom I recognized as Ella, Julia's BFF, even put a photograph of the two of them on Julia's nightstand, and Ella's favorite stuffed light brown horse on Julia's bed beside her. Behind the girls was an Irish woman with long hair who was dressed in jodhpurs, riding pinks, and tall polished black leather boots.

"Caroline!" Mom exclaimed, rising to give her a hug. "I see you brought the cowgirls." It was Coach Caroline, the woman who ran the free riding program.

Coach Caroline smiled sadly at my mother. "I was terribly sorry to hear about Julia, Charlotte. And the girls—they're absolutely devastated. They begged me to skip today's lesson to visit her and... what could I say? I know that their love of riding is strong, but their love for each other is stronger. And I love Julia, too!"

I glanced at where the girls were sharing stories about Julia, crying, and telling her how much they missed her, even though they received no response from Julia whatsoever. *They really have formed a special connection over the years,* I thought, bittersweet as it was in that moment. I thought about my own connection with Julia, and how we hadn't always gotten along. Specifically, I thought about the day I first found out about Dad losing his job, when I was so annoyed at Julia that I'd wanted to hit her with my baseball bat. How could I have even considered that—when I might not even have her for much longer?

A few minutes later, four more girls whom I recognized from Julia's class, entered the room. They too were carrying cards and flowers. After they placed their presents alongside Julia's other presents, they joined the conversation about Julia memories. Several other girls also visited before I had to leave for basketball practice. In fact, a nurse eventually came in and said, "I'm sorry, in this hospital, we don't allow this many visitors at one time. Some of you are going to have to wait in the waiting room or come back another day."

"Where is *that* rule written down?" Dad snapped, exchanging a glance with Mom. The nurse hesitated before leaving the room. I think it was comforting for my parents to see that their daughter had all these loving friends. For me personally, it was absolutely amazing. I hadn't realized Julia had so many friends.

At 5:00 p.m. sharp, my parents made me go to basketball practice. "Julia wouldn't want you to miss out on one of your favorite sports for her," they told me. I agreed, even though my heart wasn't in it.

Sure enough, when I arrived at basketball practice, Coach Elijah noticed that I looked upset. The coach was a real giant, even taller than my dad, with piercing green eyes that seemed to reduce people to half their height when he stared at them.

"What's up with you, David? You usually run onto the court with the speed of a rabbit."

I shrugged and gave him an *I'm-fine* smile—a *façade* to hide my true feelings. I didn't feel like talking about Julia. I just wanted to focus on the basketball court. However, I missed most of my shots, gave a lot of fouls during drills, and I dribbled very loosely, making it easy to cross me up. After practice, Coach Elijah called me over.

"David, please tell me what's going on. You seemed considerably off today so I have a feeling there is something you're not telling me." He gave me a gentle pat on the shoulder and gestured at the floor.

I nodded and sat down. "My—my seven-year-old sister is in the hospital in a coma!" I whimpered as I let out the whole story. My coach listened sympathetically.

After I finished, Coach said, "David, I think you, me, and most humans are similar. We can't focus when we are in trauma." Sighing, he told me his own sob story. "When I was twenty, my older brother, Jack, was killed in a horrible car crash. I was absolutely devastated. But I didn't think I could handle not playing basketball for the rest of the season. I was a starter who had led the team in scoring. I kept going to practices and games. Most of the time, I was not able to focus, so we ended up losing all our games for the rest of the season. I needed some time to mourn the loss of my brother before I could get back out there." Coach leaned down and looked me in the eyes.

"Julia's not dead yet!" I protested. "It's not like I'm actually mourning her like you were mourning your brother!

Coach Elijah gave me a small smile. "Yes, but I can see just how worried you are about her, and how that worry is affecting your concentration. Be better than me, David Kimball. Take a break from the game until you've had enough time and you're truly ready to come back. Wait until we've had at least two more games and then see if you are emotionally ready to return with your whole heart."

"But-but," I protested, as I felt my eyes watering.

"David, you are one of the most unselfish players I have—on and off the court. Staying with only half your mind on the court won't be fair to the players who have their whole mind on the court, those who want to improve and help us win," Coach told me firmly.

I looked at the ground. "I know, but Coach, I just don't think I can survive life without the sport I love!"

A thoughtful look appeared in Coach Elijah's face and he said, "I'll be right back." A minute later, he came back with a video game in a red DVD box: *HOOP-LIFE!* "If you don't have an Xbox or any game controllers, this game works fine with a regular remote-control. You can play basketball on here. In a week or so, I'll call you to see how you're handling everything, and if you feel like you're doing well enough to be able to give this game your full attention, you can come back. If not, I'll give you a little more time before checking on you again. And," Coach continued, "I'll make you a promise, in case you aren't ready to return before the season is over, David. I will save you a spot with the team next year. You won't have to try out, and I'll keep you in the lineup."

I nodded gratefully. That seemed good, and really generous. While I was certain I wouldn't be able to give basketball my complete concentration during games or practices until Julia woke up, I knew it was a very kind offer. I thanked Coach Elijah before Mom showed up and we left.

That night, I tried keeping up the *façade* with my *everything-is-fine* look, but my parents could tell I was super upset. When I told them what happened at basketball, Dad gave me a huge hug.

"Don't worry, David, just keep practicing when you're up for it and you'll still be a great basketball player," he told me gently.

I didn't like Mom's response as much. "At least you have more time to focus on schoolwork."

Meanwhile, Julia's test results—and life in general—were completely dreadful. Julia remained in a coma for about four weeks. *Four weeks!* You do not want to know how awful it is to have your little sister in a coma for four entire weeks. The worry took its toll on my schoolwork, too. I'd never paid that much attention to my studies, and my grades were seldom more than a B+; I was so worried about Julia that my grades dropped further. One class went down to the low C's. During Julia's second week in the hospital, I got two F's on tests!

The second half of January and first half of February added up to the worst month of my life. Things felt bleak. I couldn't help wondering whether or not a nefarious force had cursed us or something like that. It didn't help matters that I was looking for work wherever I could find it. There was an extremely cocky seventh grader in my school who offered me ten dollars to be his minion and do his work for him. When my parents found out, they refused to allow this. As my worry and exhaustion increased, my behavior became more and more inappropriate at school, too. I was talking back to my teachers, stamping my foot while they were talking, and other bad behavior sufficient to make at least one teacher ask, "David, why are you ridiculously rude lately?"

I still broke into uncontrollable sobs every other day, and hardly anyone could pacify me. I was also talking in garbled nonsense most of the time. My sadness about Julia made it nearly impossible to remember what class I was in! At one point I was visiting the hospital and I simply couldn't take it anymore. As I looked at her pallid face, I whimpered, "Julia, if you die, take me with you! Life will be worthless without my little sister!"

Unfortunately, my parents were nearby and overheard me. They were horrified by my declaration and berated me for it. They said they needed me, and we all had to remain positive and hopeful. I had mixed feelings about that. On one hand, most humans make crazy wishes when in pain. On the *other* hand, my parents were right. If I was going to make it through this rough time, I had to at least try to stay positive.

One thing that helped was that Julia's friends were as loyal to her as a mother. Julia always had a lot of visitors in her hospital room. It drove the nurses crazy that one of their patients always had such a crowd. I, however, was *fascinated* by it! I was so intrigued that I started taking notes. In total, there were 26 girls visiting Julia frequently, all of whom visited numerous times while Julia was unconscious. Twelve of those visitors were from Julia's riding group. Eight of them were in her class. (Shanice was the only one who was in both her class and the riding group.) Five of them were in Julia's grade in the Southeastern part of Wood Creek. The Southeast and Southwest Wood Creek kindergarten classes often took field trips to visit each other, so Julia knew them from kindergarten. Finally, two of the girls were fourth graders who were not involved with horses, whom Julia had met through Ella.

The visits meant a lot to my whole family, especially my mom. While Julia lay in that hospital bed in a coma, Mom painted a very special picture of all twenty-six of Julia's friends surrounding her bed while she slept. I couldn't look at it without tearing up.

On Valentine's Day, Julia's pals worked together to make her the most beautiful card I had ever seen! It was a giant magenta heart filled with dozens of pictures of Julia either riding horses or hanging out with them. It read:

Dear Julia,
We all miss you so, so, much! From class to riding at the stables, to swimming, to playing with our dolls, to dress making, to going to the park, nothing is the same without you! We are praying every night that our beloved sister wakes up soon. When you do, we can continue making more amazing memories with you, riding horses, swimming in Shanice's pool, or making beautiful dresses! Stay strong and remember that none of us will ever give up on you! You can knock down the wall keeping you fast asleep and rejoin the world! And we are begging you, please return soon!
Much love,

Ella, Amy, Mae, Shanice, Tara, Abby, Ariel, Genevieve, Nina, Miah, Flora, Coral, Rose, Sienna, Polly, Isabelle, Zoey, Sonia, Amanda, Phoebe, Laurel, Ruby, Sarah, Sky, Kimberly, and Harriet

The card also carried several super-sweet individual messages from some of the girls.

After Mom, Dad, and I read this gorgeous card filled with kindness, it was impossible to know which one of us was crying more. Julia's friends really cared about her and were hoping and trying to help her return. The card represented the truest love between friends that there is. Love is never futile when you're going through a hard time—like when a family member is terribly ill.

10

Slow Spring Recovery

February 17. After school, I rode my bike to the hospital with Nick, Max, and Otto. On the way, we talked about the mischievous spirit Max and his younger brother, Oliver, had shown when they played a prank on their parents. They had wreaked havoc by writing a detailed romantic love letter from one of Oliver's friend's single dads to Mrs. Clemente.

"My dad barely forgave us for that one," Max giggled, mocking his father's voice. "'Don't deny you cheated on me, Nicole!'" As a punishment, their mother banned Max and Oliver from video games and television for three weeks. We all laughed, even though, in hindsight, it was a really rotten thing to do.

Otto noticed I had fallen behind him and the others. "Dave, you okay?" he asked.

I nodded. Without basketball practice to keep me in shape, my muscles had atrophied a bit. As a result, I had lost some of my strength and speed, and I wasn't as fast a biker.

"The hospital is only a block away," Nick reminded me as I caught up.

I smiled as we pedaled calmly along the road together. When we reached the hospital, I locked my bike, waved goodbye to my friends, and went inside for my daily visit with Julia. When I passed the waiting room, I noticed my parents as well as several of Julia's friends sitting on the green sofas and smiling. That was odd. Normally, when my parents or Julia's posse arrived at the hospital, they went straight to her hospital room. And while smiles weren't as rare, sadness and tears were definitely more common. Something was up. Suddenly Mom—whose hazel eyes are as strong in sight as they are pretty—laser focused on me and dashed to greet me.

"David, guess what? Julia may have woken up!" she exclaimed joyfully. *What? Yes!!* "Julia can now open her eyes and has blurted out a few words. The doctors are currently examining her."

After what seemed like an eternity, a nurse entered the waiting room. "Mr. and Mrs. Kimball? Julia has in fact woken up, and the world is probably looking very unfamiliar to her. She needs familiar voices to talk to her. Could one of you please come with me into Julia's room?"

"I'll do it," I exclaimed at once. I needed to see this for myself.

The nurse raised a blond eyebrow, taken aback by my fervor. She glanced at my parents, who nodded their permission. "Okay, David, come with me." She led me into Julia's hospital room.

Even though I had seen Julia the day before, her room seemed different to me. Julia's crisp white hospital bed sheets had been replaced with her own soft pink sheets from home. Julia's horse pictures had been packed away. Ever since Julia first came to the hospital, her bed had been filled with stuffed animals. Now, most of the plush toys sat in a cardboard box, leaving only her friend Ella's favorite plush horse and a stuffed blue whale that Julia gripped in her little hands. The doctors must have been trying to make the world look less big and confusing by stowing away unnecessary items. There were still ghastly saline bags rigged to Julia intravenously, and feeding tubes. I hoped all the tubes and needles wouldn't scare her. But the orange breathing tube Julia had been wearing all month was gone! Noting its absence, I assumed happily that she was breathing properly again. *Hooray*!

The nurse stood back. "Talk to her," she whispered.

I examined Julia. Her pretty hazel eyes were flickering around the room and her mouth was wide open.

"Julia?" I spoke softly, still, she did not seem to be aware of me.

"D-D-D-D-D-Dolphin?" she stammered looking at me. I laughed. Julia was trying to remember my name!

"David!" I corrected her. "I'm your big brother! Dolphins are beautiful curvy sea animals with a fin on their back."

"Sea? I see, I see—white, brown, blue..." Julia listed all the colors she could see before closing her eyes, exhausted from the effort, and falling into a deep slumber. I couldn't believe what I'd just witnessed! I felt like Christmas had arrived ten months early!

That evening, my family stayed in the hospital overnight, as we frequently did. I was sitting on a comfortable recliner chair next to Julia's bed struggling to fall asleep. As I closed my eyes, I listened to my parents discuss my sister.

"She's awake and she's alive," Dad remarked, in awe.

"Her muscles have weakened since the fainting, and her brain has not yet recovered fully," Mom replied quietly.

"Nurse Bellamy says that the doctors have to run more tests and give Julia therapy to refresh her memory before she will be truly ready to come back to us. Her prognosis is good, though. They say she is remembering words and names more quickly than the hospital had expected!" Dad said. He seemed to glow, and his pearly white smile was bigger than I'd seen it in a while. "Oh, Charlotte," he squealed, tears of joy leaking from his eyes, "if we can get our baby fully recovered, maybe anything is possible! There's hope I'll be working again someday soon, and maybe we'll even have a proper home again!"

"I hope so," said Mom, sitting down in the wooden chair by the door. "We *will* get everything back someday, Harry. We have to!"

As I listened to their happy conversation, I, too, felt full of hope. *Could the curse of homelessness really not be my family's fate forever?*

About ten days after Julia awoke from the coma, the doctors allowed her to come home to us at the inn. I was worried we would have to do a lot of cleaning of our very messy room so Julia could recover in peace. But the doctors reassured us that Julia was sufficiently recovered to be able to thrive in a busy family atmosphere.

Even though she still spent most of her time sleeping, Julia's memory was making tremendous progress. Her recollection of language—and *life*—was coming back fast. By March, she was caught up enough to have lengthy conversations with others, even though she would then need to sleep for a long time. Her vocabulary and ability to engage with the family—such as asking Dad to play horses with her or requesting cookies for dessert—seemed to be just as advanced and normal as any conversation a seven-year-old-girl would have!

However, things were still far from perfect for Julia. At school, she had a lot of catching up to do, having missed a month and a half. She couldn't go back to classes yet so everyone agreed that she would be homeschooled for the rest of the year. Also, the doctors still would not let her go anywhere more exciting than the Public Library. That was tough because it meant no hanging out at the stables and no suspenseful movies. The specialists at the hospital encouraged her to watch home videos of family trips and holidays to help her recover her memory.

In April, there was a town carnival at which Taylor Swift was giving a performance, at the invitation of the Governor of Ohio, who had some personal ties to Wood Creek. Taylor Swift was Julia's favorite singer, and *Wildest Dreams* was her favorite song. You can imagine how heartbroken Julia felt that she couldn't attend (plus, we could not have afforded the tickets anyway). Oh, how dark her mood was throughout the day of the carnival. Unexpectedly, Justin bought me a ticket and I was able to go to the carnival with my video camera and shoot a video for Julia of *Wildest* Dreams being performed. She was thrilled and adored the video.

Not long after, baseball season started, and things went really well. The Wood Creek Baseball League works the same way as the basketball league, and I made the

Level 2 Team. Thankfully, my atrophied muscles were recovering from my hiatus from working out. Justin, Robby, Max, Louis, and Will were also on the team. While I didn't get a lot of playing time on the field, I did have several highlights that season, including countless great catches, four singles, six doubles, five triples, and even a homerun!

By April, Julia was well enough that she could be a bit more physically active. She often spent afternoons going on walks with Mom (and sometimes Dad, when Mom could convince him to come). Frequently, they would pass the bright green park where I practiced baseball and I would wave. Julia still had to strap on a brace every day. She camouflaged it by wearing a dress. I was happy to notice her legs seemed to be gaining strength as she limped less and less each time she walked by the baseball field. Because she was still recovering, Julia seldom had friends over. However, some of the girls in her riding squad visited almost every weekend to massage Julia's legs and arms and try to speed up her progress with laughter and chatter.

"The goal is to get you back as quickly as possible," Ella noted briskly as she pulled on Julia's leg. "Next year, I'm going to be too old to stay in Caroline's Cowgirls! I don't want my last few days with the squad to be without *you*!" However, by the time their last riding show rolled around, Julia didn't seem ready to be back at either the barn or at school.

"The show is a week away," Mom intoned cautiously.

Good news came when the doctors felt that Julia was finally ready to go to events like movies, plays, concerts, and my baseball games. So Julia would at least be allowed to watch the equestrian competition at the horse farm.

"There's still a time, Julia," Ella told her the week before the show, as she stretched Julia's leg. "Anything can happen in a week."

"You're pulling my leg," Julia replied, giggling. I was glad her silly humor was back in full force.

"Don't give up!" insisted Ella, "You *are* going to be in the show." Little did I know, a plan was hatching in Julia's brain.

On May 12th at 1:30 p.m., Julia, Mom, Dad, and I sat in the bleachers at Carmelo Stables watching the girls show off their equestrian skills. Glancing over at Julia, I could sense something in her pouty smile. It was almost as if she was pretending to be sad. She had that familiar look of twinkly determination in her eyes that she got when she was about to get into some kind of mischief and didn't want to get caught!

"Mom, may I go to the bathroom?" Julia asked nonchalantly.

Mom nodded, and Julia meandered off. She seemed to be walking very slowly which I found odd, since lately she had been more energetic by the day.

"You want me to go with her, Mom?"

"She needs to feel like we believe she can get around by herself, David," cautioned Mom, laying her hand on my arm to keep me in my seat.

I watched Julia walk across the manicured lawn of the equestrian estate and then alongside the stables before disappearing around the corner. I knew that Julia knew perfectly well that the bathrooms were located on the *opposite* side of the stables.

"*Y'aa!!* Great jump!" yelled Mom, as Julia's friend, Shannon Allen, hurtled her horse over the blue block in front of the bleachers.

"Yes!" Louis exclaimed behind me, applauding for his sister. We high-fived.

"She's doing great, Louis!" I told him, smiling.

That's when I heard a click and the sound of hooves trotting. The *clippity-clop* wasn't coming from the black pony right in front of us in the ring—nor any from the horses trotting around the arena. The hoof beats came from the barn. In that moment, I didn't think much of it. I just continued watching the girls and their horses doing jumps.

"Louis, did you get that new MLB video game?" I asked.

Louis nodded. "And I'm game to beat you at it any day, David!"

"We'll see!" I smirked.

That's when we heard a horse hooves bolting so quickly it sounded like a Barry Allen (a.k.a. *the Flash*) version of a horse! That was quite a surprise, since the other girls with their horses had elegantly walked their horses from the barn to the arena. As the girl rode out, she looked kind of familiar.

A few seconds later, the girl shouted, "Let's go, Melba!" and she and horse sprinted into the arena. I suddenly realized who it was!

"Julia!" I exclaimed.

"My baby!" Mom squealed, a hand covering her mouth as the parents of Caroline's other Cowgirls in the bleachers whispered to each other in wonder.

"Is that Julia?"

"How's that possible? She just got out of a coma recently!"

"Guess she's better now!"

"Such a strong rider!"

By now all eyes were on Julia. She leaned forward with her back parallel to Melba's neck. She was near enough that I could see her place her hands at the center of Melba's mane, gripping close to the roots. She still held the reins, not tightly, but enough that there was no slack. A moment later, Julia's horse made one of the most amazing jumps I had ever seen—graceful and powerful, and Julia's form was elegantly poised. Galloping calmly yet quickly over the blue jump, Julia and Melba landed with a gentle *plop!* Then Julia rode around the track to a cheering audience. I was amazed at how easily Julia managed her horse. I had tried riding horses before and found that directing the horse where to go was hard for me. I never had Julia's passion for horses. When Julia came closer, I noticed her left leg; she had removed her brace in the stables! At first that made me nervous. However, as I looked closer, I saw how much stronger her leg had become over the past six weeks of physical therapy.

The girls in Julia's riding group clapped and chanted: "Julia! Julia!"

The crowd joined in. Julia even leaned into Melba's sunflower-yellow mane and joined in the chanting of her own name. (I can only guess that she wanted to make it sound like Melba could talk and was chanting "Julia!" too.)

My parents didn't seem to know what to make of what had just happened. They were whispering about what consequence to give Julia for doing something dangerous when her body was still recovering. Yet I could tell that their pride and happiness had won out over any kind of reprimand. Then, Julia rode Melba toward the stables where Coach Caroline waited outside with her hands on her hips. I wondered what *she* thought of the whole thing. The two of them spoke for a bit. Caroline's hands gestured a lot; Julia nodded several times. Caroline hugged Julia, then my little sister rode back to the arena for a triumphant gallop around it. After she dismounted, her partner in crime, Ella, came and led the pony away, and—beaming—Julia joined us on the bleachers. Later, we learned that Ella had saddled up Melba to have her waiting for Julia when she sneaked off to the barn.

"Are you in trouble with your coach?" I asked.

"Coach Caroline wasn't upset at me for crashing the performance at all! She loved it!" Julia smiled joyfully.

"I'm very proud of you, sweetie," Mom whispered, wrapping Julia in a hug. "While you should next time ask before doing something this dangerous, I think your health is completely back!"

Mom and Dad whispered between them before Dad turned to Julia and asked, "So, Julia, you think you're ready to go back to school?"

Julia's pretty smile grew twice its normal size, and her hazel eyes shone. "I'm up for anything, Dad!" she exclaimed and gave him a hug.

Nevertheless, after her *performance*, Julia slept for two days straight. The doctors were a little annoyed that Julia had done something this risky without their consent while she was still recovering. They excoriated my parents, noting "clumsy parenting skills." In the end, however, they gave their blessing. The following Monday, Julia entered the shiny bright red door of Southwest Wood Creek Elementary School for the first time in months!

That Thursday, I was in for quite a surprise! My old elementary school nemesis, Alexa Brewer—for whose mother my mother was still doing housekeeping—approached me in Spanish class.

"David, I heard about Julia's big horseback riding performance!" she told me, her voice full of genuine happiness. "I heard our moms talking about it, and I'm really happy Julia's well again! I was really worried about her. Congratulations and good luck!"

I was taken aback. Was this the same Alexa who had made my life miserable since kindergarten? Was this the same Alexa who had made denigrating remarks to me every chance she got for six years? I didn't even know how to respond.

"Th—thanks, Alexa," I stammered, raising my hand to meet the high-five she offered me enthusiastically.

That June, on Julia's eighth birthday, we had a huge party for her at our church—its women's club pooled money to cover the cost of the celebration. The day was extra special as we hadn't been sure Julia would live to be eight, and Mom insisted that I give a talk. So just before Dad was about to cut the apple pie he had made for Julia, I read a speech I wrote for my beloved little sister. I told them about how terrible it had been to find out Julia was in the hospital and to leave her there for a month, and how Julia recovered from her coma with an amazing amount of strength! Tearfully, I thanked God for sparing Julia and wished my beloved sister a happy birthday! I think even the loftiest academics and vainest snobs in our church were amazed that an eleven-year-old wrote such a sophisticated speech. However, in spite of all my pride, I only had one thing left on my mind: *pie*. And just at that moment, my dad carried out a big birthday apple pie. We sang *Happy Birthday,* and I was among the first to grab a big fat slice—with a huge scoop of vanilla ice cream. It was delicious!

After we ate, we watched a puppet show about horses that could sew. (Mom had painted the puppet show background.) After the horses finished sewing their outfits, they had a hilarious costume party. The Shetland pony dressed as a fairy. A Palomino horse dressed as a canary. The Corsican horse was a scarecrow and stood completely still during the entire party. It was very funny, and by the end of it, the guests were laughing loudly. A few elders, whose children were friends with Mom and Dad, mocked it for making little sense, with narrow-minded comments like, "Horses can't sew! Horses can't talk! Horses don't throw parties!" (*Um, it's called having an imagination*! I thought.) However, those humorless elders' opinions didn't matter, because everyone else loved it.

11

Camp Poverty Escape

By the time I finished fifth grade, there was no question that my family was on the move and inspired to focus on success. After the painful experience of Julia nearly losing her life, we all wanted to make sure that that could not happen again—to any of us. And in order to do that, we needed more money. Dad needed to find a job, even if that meant moving to another town, which until now, my parents had resisted in order to keep Julia and me in the same excellent school system and avoid further disruption for us. It was hard enough for Dad to forgive himself, and we weren't sure if the patrons in our town would ever forgive Dad either for letting a drug addict work at his restaurant, and for that little girl having been kidnapped by said employee. One thing we knew for sure was that we could not—*would* not—stay *in the hole* forever.

Dad's alcoholism was still a serious issue. Although he didn't drink nearly as much as a year ago, he still drank more than he should, so he didn't feel ready to look for a job. The alcohol was also making him depressed; he knew he was out of control. His downward spiral was further worsened by the rejection he faced the last time he went searching for a job. In my opinion, Dad had become a little paranoid from the overall effects of alcohol in his mind and body. He thought that everyone in town would just refuse to hire him or even do business in a place where he worked again, just like last time.

Thankfully, he was increasing the amount of time he spent at Alcoholics Anonymous meetings. He kept a journal open for Mom to fact check, and I snooped and saw that every day he was talking to his *AA sponsor*. Mom said this person was helping Dad by providing a kind of check-and-balance system, and that Dad was working extra hard to stop his drinking. Meanwhile, my mom used her wits to convince Mrs. Brewer (mother of my old enemy Alexa) to increase her salary. I also tried to convince Mom to sell her paintings to earn money. Her insecure reply was, "My paintings aren't good enough to be sold, David. I don't think anyone would buy them."

"You can still try," I argued.

Mom refused. Even though she loved painting, she was still shy about her work.

As for me, Mom knew that I was a hard worker, and she decided to put me to work for the summer. After doing some research, she found a camp in the Adirondack Mountains for impoverished kids ages eleven and up. Apparently, the camp was known for training kids in little jobs that would help them earn money for their family. It was called Camp Poverty Escape or Camp P.E. The number of spots available at the camp was limited, in part because the camp paid for everything, including transportation to and from the camp. Because of that, my mom signed me up immediately.

It was pretty cool, I thought, that the woman who founded the camp had herself once been homeless, before she gradually rebuilt her life by working her way out of *the hole*. She wanted other kids to have the same chance at a better life than she had had. And so she saved money by selling flowers, old pots, junk, and jewelry, as well as playing piano and singing for sell-out crowds. After years of working hard, the founder had raised enough money to open up the camp. And she got grants and donations from various sources, too.

Soon after school got out, I prepared to leave for camp. As I packed the suitcase I'd borrowed from Justin, Mom kept harping on me about little things. "Don't forget your toothbrush! Or your floss! Make sure you pack books! I know you don't love reading that much, but you must read over the summer!"

By the time I got to the train station, I was full of excitement for my journey to start. The train was drafty and slow. I didn't care; I was happy that I was about to have an experience that might be the catalyst to propel my life out of poverty!

For lunch, I ate the chicken sandwich Mom had packed—as I watched the little boy next to me eat two hot dogs from the train's restaurant car. Two train hot dogs!! I felt extremely jealous. What I'd have given to be able to afford even *one*. For a brief moment, I had the urge to throw my sandwich at him, but I knew my mom would say such a thing was rude and "not something God would want"—so, I enjoyed the thought impishly and decided against chucking my lunch in his face as I watched him devour his hot dogs.

Plus, it's not like the kid was a bad person. He saw my copy of *Heat* and it turned out he liked Mike Lupica too! We ended up talking the whole ride about our favorite Mike Lupica books.

When the train arrived in the Adirondack Mountains, a counselor in a green "*Camp P.E.*" t-shirt met me, and we traveled a short distance by taxi to the camp. As we drove through the campus, I noticed its clean, beautiful green lawns, and a couple of big houses. One was blue and had a yellow sign that read, "*Home.*" The other was orange, with a red sign that read, "*Jobs & Activities.*" As I stepped out of the taxi in front of the main building, I felt the summer sun warming me up, and a cool breeze blew through my hair.

A tall, smiling Black woman with glasses and a head full of curly black hair approached the taxi.

"Welcome, welcome!" she exclaimed, shaking my hand after she thanked the driver. "Now, which camper are *you*? And how old are you?"

"My—my name is David Kimball and I'm eleven," I replied shyly. "What's your name?"

"Welcome, David! My name is Counselor Niasha, and I'm the founder of Camp P.E." It occurred to me that she was the one who had built herself out of homelessness and done all that work to create the camp, and suddenly I felt awestruck. The woman continued to smile as she checked what I assumed was my name off her list. "It's very nice to meet you, David. Your mother told me you love basketball and baseball." I nodded eagerly. Her smile dazzled me. "And do I remember correctly that you enjoy video games and movies, and have a slight interest in writing?"

"It's all true," I confirmed, grinning.

Counselor Niasha asked a couple more questions before telling me, in a patient, lighthearted voice, "David, welcome to Camp Poverty Escape. It's just about dinner time and we eat dinner in our home building. See the sign?" I nodded. Briefly, Niasha explained how breakfast, dinner, sleeping, and free time were held in the *Home* dormitory, while morning and afternoon activities and lunch were held in the *Jobs & Activities* building. "Do you understand?" she asked gently. I nodded, and Counselor Niasha continued in her low voice, "Okay, David. In that case, welcome once again, and enjoy your dinner." She pointed in the direction I should go.

I dragged my suitcase with me across the grass to the *Home* building and went inside. The Dining Room/Kitchen lay to the left. Boy did it smell good! The aroma of sweet potatoes, rice, hot dogs, squash, green beans, almonds, and muffins filled my nose, along with the fragrance of pineapples and blackberries. Other than perhaps on Halloween, or maybe at an occasional party or sleepover, never had this many dinner options been presented to me—not in years! In the dining room, there were about fifty hungry kids as young as me and as old as seventeen.

I noticed a lot of differences among the kids' backgrounds. For example, there seemed to be equal numbers of Black kids, Hispanic kids, and White kids. It seemed cool to me that Camp P.E. was such a diverse place. In Wood Creek, well over half of the town was White, and the remainder of the town's population was made up of many other ethnicities. Another thing I noticed was that although a few tables were all guys or all girls, a significant portion of the tables were co-ed. I found that interesting, especially since ever since elementary school, at my school, boys and girls typically did not sit with each other during lunch.

There was also diversity among the activity. Some kids were talking, others were reading, and some were playing cards. There were even differences in the number of people at each table! There were tables that held 10-15 people and others held smaller groups. And a few kids sat by themselves. I liked how there were so many differences in so many people in one room.

I left my suitcase behind a chair in the spacious vestibule where other kids' suitcases were strewn along the walls. I got in line, grabbed a tray, and loaded it with green beans, hot dogs, and sweet potatoes. As I went to find a place to eat, I noticed that most of the kids were teenagers, and I suddenly felt very shy. I was pretty sure most of the kids weren't newbies like me and already had friends, and I figured they wouldn't want a new little kid sitting with them. Plus, I looked even younger because of my height.

After wandering around for a few minutes with little success, I found a table with one kid about my age who sat reading a book about the Mexican-American War. In all honesty, it was not her book that first caught my eye. She was a beautiful girl with almond eyes, and long black hair. And let's face it, who doesn't like to look at someone that pretty? Although—why anyone would want to read a book about a historical event with that much carnage, I could not figure out.

"May I sit here?" I asked shyly.

When the girl looked up from her book, I could tell from the look in her eyes that she was bright, and not just a pretty face.

"Hmm? Sure," she replied. She had a soft quiet voice. As I sat down across from her, she put away her book. "I'm Gloria."

"I'm David," I replied as I munched on my beans, "David Kimball."

"Gloria Zayes." She held out her smooth light brown hand. I shook it as a nearby TV began to play a Wildcats-Giants game. "Let's go Wildcats! Play ball!" I cried out louder than I had intended to. I blushed.

Gloria smiled at me. "You like baseball?" she asked, interested.

I nodded. "Baseball and basketball are my life!" I told her.

Gloria's almond eyes widened. "I love basketball too! I play it every day!"

Immediately, we talked about our favorite teams, the Cavaliers and the Bulls. We also talked about drills in basketball jargon, such as PR-right. After I finished my dinner, I went to get a muffin as Gloria finished her meal. And when I got back, I saw she'd returned to her book.

She whispered to herself a bit, saying loud enough for me to hear her, "Oh, this soldier had on his epitaph, *All I wanted was to return to my family.*"

I sat down and ate my muffin waiting for Gloria to look up at me, and when she finally did a few minutes later, she blushed bright red. "I—I'm sorry, David. I tend to get so involved in books, I forget the real world exists and I don't always bother to check if who I'm sitting with is still there!"

I laughed. "Oh, don't worry about it, Gloria. I'm the same way with TV!"

We shared a good chuckle, and went on talking about sports, our families, and other things for about an hour. Gloria and I had a lot in common. We were both eleven and going into sixth grade. We both came from religious families and we both had mothers whom we adored. We both had an eight-year-old sibling. We both loved basketball. And, of course, we were both currently homeless.

Gloria unexpectedly told me about how when she was six, she faced a horrible experience where a group of White men (Gloria's family was Hispanic) barged into her house and brutally beat up her father. They were racists who did not want Hispanic people living in their neighborhood. Gloria knew this, because right when the lowlifes barged in, the first thing they did was shout, "You taco-heads have no right to live in our hood!"

"*Mami* and my brother, Juan, were out," Gloria explained. "It was just me and *Papà* in the house. I tried to call the police, but one of the men grabbed my phone and locked me in the bathroom where I watched them through the keyhole as they attacked poor *Papà*. After ten minutes, blood had drenched *Papà's* shirt, and his arms were badly scratched. At that point, one of the men told *Papà*, 'Stand over us with the sharpest knife in this house, or else I'll shoot you.' The man tapped his pocket where he was probably carrying a pistol. What choice did *Papà* have? The attackers then lay down and bit and scratched themselves all over. One of them made an overdramatic police call, telling the cops that *Papà* had invited them over before going crazy and now he was attacking them! Within minutes, the police arrived and arrested *Papà* and charged him with assault and attempted murder charges! It was not a fair court decision as the jury was made up of an all-White and all-male jury, against a Latino man—yes, in the *Twenty-First Century*—and my father was sentenced to thirty years in prison!" Gloria told me about how her family had to move from Virginia to Maryland to get away without ever looking back.

"Why didn't any neighbors come to help?" I asked.

Gloria rolled her eyes and actually spat at the ground. "Because my whole town was filled with racist monsters who didn't see me and my family as human beings, because of our skin color!" She scowled. "And they couldn't stand the idea that people of color would have as much or more money than they did."

We had finished eating and decided to go into the spacious living room, which turned out to be a cozy place. The walls were full of pictures of people who had moved our world forward, including a faded portrait of Benjamin Franklin. There were four yellow tables, and half a dozen beautiful, colorful couches. Teenagers sat around everywhere watching TV, chatting, reading, or playing cards or chess.

As we entered the camp living room, Gloria continued to tell me about her life.

"Months after my father was arrested, on the day I turned seven—" sniffling, Gloria's voice broke off, then she explained that tragedy struck again on her birthday! I pointed at two empty stools for us near the fireplace. It wasn't burning; still, it looked nice and was away from other kids. "My mom was never the same after what happened to *Papà*. And some days, she got very worked up thinking about her sadness so that she just couldn't concentrate. So, that night, with me in the back seat, *Mami* was driving with her tears clouding her sight, and next thing you know—a disastrous car crash! I was all right, but *Mami*—she broke her spine, and could no longer walk! She lost her job and couldn't work." Gloria paused and let a few tears drop before whispering sadly, "I was barely past second grade when we lost our home and had to move into a couple of spare rooms at our church."

She went on to tell me more about her father who, she said, had been good at sports, smart, hardworking, and very good-looking. *Like my dad before substance abuse*, I thought, identifying with Gloria's pain. I told her about my own struggles, such as the night my parents and I slept in the rain after our car was stolen. I also told her about having my father become an alcoholic, and how Julia had been in a coma for a month. Gloria was also very sympathetic when I talked about Julia, telling me she couldn't imagine Juan—her brother—being in a coma.

Over the next few days, Gloria continued to tell me about her life, and I learned about the happy part of Gloria's story. I found out that even though she lost her home and her father, Gloria still had the strength to build herself up from practically nothing and *"Thrive*, with a capital T!" as she said. Her parents may have lost their ability to prosper and succeed, yet their misfortune impelled Gloria to feel that she was their only hope and she had to live the life her parents had lost. She had a lot of friends, she was a great basketball player, she played piano, and she took school very seriously. Gloria was an all-star in her English, History, and Spanish classes. She even studied those subjects in her free time—something I could not believe anyone would do!

Gloria gestured me over to a nearby piano. "You want to hear me play?" She was smiling eagerly. I grinned at her and gave a thumbs up. Gloria sat on the piano stool and played *Imagine* by John Lennon. The lyrics were very inspiring, and Gloria was a great singer and pianist. She sang with such confidence; it was very impressive. By the end of that melodious mix of Gloria's gorgeous voice, and the piano's beautiful low tones, I was on my feet clapping in amazement. I had never really cared much for music up until that point, but it was impossible *not* to be in love with Gloria's strong, raw talent!

"Gloria, that was amazing! Well done!" I told her enthusiastically.

Gloria grinned. "Thanks, David," she said, giving me a high five. "Thank you for not acting weird or going all—" Gloria made a hysterical face. She squinted her eyes, she stuck out her tongue, and her left nostril closed in a little. I burst out laughing and stuck out my tongue back at her, while I gave myself bunny ears. We continued to try and make each other laugh until a tall, bearded, red-haired counselor entered the living room. This man, Counselor Terry, reminded us that a long night's sleep was essential for a good new day, and it would help us work better and be more successful in helping our families emerge out of poverty—something he would repeat every night at camp at bedtime.

I felt pretty comfortable about meeting my roommate. I figured, *whatever he's like, whoever he is, bring him forward!* After I opened the bedroom door, I noticed that the scene in my room was quite different from what I was expecting. It seemed the new roommate had decided to keep the whole room for himself. Already, he had taped up posters of macabre zombies around most of the room. And to my surprise, my roommate was asleep *under* his bed. I decided to deal with introductions in the morning. After I brushed my teeth at the little sink in our room, I got under my covers, pulled out a piece of paper and a flashlight and wrote a letter to Mom, Dad, and Julia. When I was midway through writing, my roommate suddenly pulled his head out from under his bed.

"Who's there?" he asked in a feisty voice. Feeling a little nervous, I stayed quiet. The voice persisted, "Who else is in this room? Show yourself and you can have a bag of candy!"

I flashed my light at him and smiled and told him my name. "What's your name?"

A tall spider monkey of a boy with dark blond hair emerged from beneath his bed and stood up straight. He reminded me a bit of Nick, except Nick is awfully pale and has broad lips, whereas this guy was tan with more compact lips. He looked about thirteen.

"I'm Danny," he told me. He passed me a bag of M&M's. As I munched, Danny talked to me about horror movies, before we both went to bed.

I decided that Danny was a good guy, very interesting and funny, even if a little strange. I had asked him, "Why do you like zombies?"

He'd shrugged and said, "Haunted things and killers are cool."

When I told Gloria about him the next morning, she replied, "I know what his epitaph is going to be: *Now that I'm dead, I want to be in a horror show!*"

"From now on," I told Gloria, "to reduce bedtime stress, I'll have to spend the evening time before lights out reading in order to avoid Danny's wacky horror stories." She laughed.

Then, before breakfast, Gloria and I went outside to play basketball until the kitchen opened up. I thought this would be easy. I didn't even think it was possible to lose against a girl. Not to mention, I was an incredible player who was going into sixth grade, yet I could play as well as an eighth grader. My mom has dozens of pictures—and paintings for that matter—of me taking foul shots, dribbling, and guarding to show off my natural talent. However, Gloria stunned me. She pretty much flew all over the court taking shot after shot from wherever, not to mention, throwing in a couple tricks like dribbling between her legs. I scored too, and I tried my best, but Gloria was super fast and super strong. I could barely keep my game up. And she won 55 - 47 by the time we were called in for breakfast.

"Can you teach me some of your moves?" I asked Gloria as we both got about half a dozen pancakes for breakfast.

"Absolutely!" Gloria agreed. I looked forward to it!

Soon, it was time to get into the day's planned activities. When I saw the camp's list of activities available for 11-year-olds, I wasn't completely sure that it would work for me. There was no sports coaching, or anything related to sports for my age. That was disappointing, since I thought that would be my best way to earn money. I chose babysitting and cooking for my first week. I like younger children and I thought maybe I could teach a couple of kids how to play sports. I chose cooking because my dad had been a cook and I thought it would be cool to follow in his footsteps. I was delighted to learn that Gloria was also taking babysitting for the first week. What wasn't nearly as delightful, however, was the counselor's reaction when we got distracted by our conversation on our way to babysitting practice and we arrived late. Once we arrived, the counselor, a woman with green glasses and raven black hair, with a nametag that read *Counselor Kristy*, frowned at us.

"What are your names, Late-People?" asked Counselor Kristy. After Gloria and I introduced ourselves, Counselor Kristy told us, "Rule Number One: It is not good to be late for work, especially for babysitting jobs. The parents probably won't be happy because you'll probably be making *them* late for wherever they are headed. Being late will tarnish your reputation with parents. They will consider you irresponsible and probably not hire you again, except perhaps as a last resort. From now on, you will be on time for babysitting practice to train you to be on time for your babysitting jobs."

Gloria and I exchanged an uncomfortable, slightly ashamed glance before muttering in unison, "Sorry."

Despite her strictness, what Counselor Kristy had said made sense. I appreciated her motivating us to be better and more professional.

In spite of the not great start, I did well with babysitting practice. I took notes about tips for babysitting (*memorize facts about the kids you sit for; instead of watching TV when sitting, pay attention to the kids; be prepared to play a lot of games and chase them around and make them laugh, and feed them healthful food*), and when I took my first test for the activity, I got an A+. (*Yes!*)

A couple of weeks later, the camp gave me a real babysitting job for a family with two children, the Harrises. They had a five-year-old boy, Ian, and a three-year-old girl, Annie. The children were adorable, and I had loads of fun with them, playing games like *Candy Land* and *Chutes and Ladders*. I also taught them how to make sandwiches, though I was careful not to have our lessons involve knives at all. I also read the kids stories and bathed them. When the kids were asleep, I even did housework because the camp counselors talked a lot about doing more than what was asked of you! The Harris parents were very surprised when they saw how much I had done, and even paid me extra.

One thing the camp taught us that was definitely useful was how to save money. At the end of every week, we were paid around twenty-five dollars. In the second week, several campers depleted all the money they had earned when they went off to a nearby candy store! Our counselors were furious and gave us a huge lecture about how important saving is.

Counselor Niasha actually roared at us, saying, "Even if your family wasn't struggling through poverty, it is beyond impractical and selfish to spend fifty dollars on candy! In this camp, we are careful with our money. And anyone who thinks it is okay to be wasteful can pack their bags and leave immediately!"

I also learned about *resumé* writing. During the fourth week of camp, all the campers took a *resumé* writing class, and were taught to include all of our accomplishments and skills. Next, we learned how to write a cover letter to a potential employer. I enjoyed writing letters about the skills I had that made me a good fit for the job.

I had had a lot of practice writing letters already, writing home a letter every four days. I wrote a lot of letters to Justin too. This was the first summer the two of us had spent apart in five years, and I missed him a lot! We came up with a crazy plan to convince the whole camp to go to Hawaii where Justin was staying with his family, but we never got the chance.

As Gloria and I spent more and more time together, I couldn't help feeling slightly like I was cheating on Justin. I know, being *besties* doesn't work in the same way *relationships* do, and besides, I had always shared him with Robby. Now, however, it still felt kind of funny. Especially when we had an Independence Day barbeque, and Gloria asked, "What do you want to eat, Camp-Bestie?" I blushed and Gloria looked at me nervously. "I mean, we're best-camp-friends David, aren't we?" she asked shyly.

I hesitated and gave an equivocal answer, "Gloria, that's an interesting question."

Gloria giggled. "You're funny," she told me. "Now stop being evasive and answer me. Are we or are we not?"

I decided to give another answer that was only slightly less clear that might make her understand I was worried that I was "cheating on" Justin.

"Do you have a best friend in Maryland?" I asked.

Gloria nodded. "Her name is Brianna. She's awesome!" Gloria told me. "I was feeling cynical about whether or not I could survive after we moved into the church and Brianna told me, 'You can do it! Your parents may have lost their success, but you can right that wrong!' Her words helped me strive to succeed at anything I put my mind to, and I always appreciated her wisdom." She added, "Are you worried about me replacing a best friend from home?" I nodded. Gloria giggled and shook her head. "Don't worry, David. There is nothing wrong with having two best friends."

"In that case," I told her firmly and unequivocally, as I looked straight into her gorgeous brown eyes, "I think we are definitely not just best-camp-friends, but actual best friends!"

Gloria's face lit up. "Yay!" she squealed, giving me a tight squeeze. We both got hot soup in a thermos and slices of watermelon and pizza, before Counselor Terry got up to speak.

"Ladies and Gentlemen, we have a guest speaker who has an important announcement to share."

A tall man with black hair in a fancy dark suit came into the center of the room.

"Hi, everyone. My name is Jim Powell!" With his eyes full of power, Mr. Powell gave a speech that really surprised me. "I was never a camper or counselor here, but because I was homeless for a couple of years and because I've visited here before to give speeches, I feel a strong connection to this place. That is also because I feel like I have something to share.

"I know life can look frustrating and bleak. Trust me, though, it doesn't have to be! We all can succeed and thrive!"

I nudged Gloria and whispered, "There's *your* word, *Thrive*."

"With a capital *T*," she whispered back.

"This is America, the place where dreams come true!" Mr. Powell continued, "You all *will* escape the shackles of poverty. You just have to believe in yourselves, work hard, and try your best! Through all that, you will achieve financial success and homes. No one can be forced to struggle forever. If you work hard, care about others, and be consistent, you will make it! Thank you, and good luck! Most important, *don't ever give up!*" Everyone burst into applause. That was quite an encouraging speech!

"Wow, he's a good speaker!" Gloria remarked as she took yet another slice of pizza oozing with sauce, "I wish I could be as elegant and self-confident as he is," she added, "Powell's epitaph will be, *Don't ever give up*."

I chuckled. "Gloria, just out of curiosity, why are you obsessed with epitaphs?"

Gloria shrugged. "I guess, it's cool to see what people's legacies are after they die," she said. "And I'm worried about mine. David, I don't want to let my parents down after all they've lost..." Her eyes filled with tears, and I remembered the sad story she had told me about her parents.

"You will please them," I told her kindly. "You are really smart and talented! You have a lot going for you,

Gloria Zayes!" I put my arm around her and let her cry into my shoulder. She looked up at me and smiled a little before she continued crying. Feeling dreamy, I almost kissed her. Despite any feelings I might have had for her, I knew we were probably better off as friends. "C'mon, eat," I told Gloria. "So we can go shoot hoops."

Gloria shook her head. "I think I ate too much pizza," she admitted, "I should probably just go to bed. See you tomorrow, David."

Red-eyed, she walked off and I finished my dinner alone before going to my own room. There, I wrote another letter to my family. I also wrote to Justin. I considered tricking Justin into believing that Gloria had forced me to be her best friend. Then I decided it wasn't worth it and realized he would know Gloria wasn't replacing him. Then, before any more thoughts of what to say or do to my best friend occurred to me, I fell fast asleep. I knew both friendships would always be more than just a part of my life. They were my brother and sister, and I would always care for both of them.

In the fifth week at Camp P.E., everyone had to take a business course. In it, each kid was told to come up with a business idea and learn how to advertise it before spending week six (the last week) actually running the business there in the Adirondacks. Gloria and I chose to team up to teach little kids, ages five to eight, how to play basketball. In our advertisement, we wrote about our skills with children and how good we were at basketball. We also went door to door giving out our fliers and, with Counselor Niasha's help, we wrote an advertisement and Camp P.E. paid for it to be placed in the local *Adirondack Daily Enterprise*. We also got a shared email account to make it possible for parents to email us to sign up their children. We also asked Counselor Niasha's permission to use the gym for our mini-camp, and she agreed.

During the final week of Camp P.E., we ran our little camp teaching about twelve little kids how to play basketball. Gloria and I were both very happy that we had an equal number of girls and boys. We taught them how to pivot, take foul shots, do drills, and more. We focused most of all on team spirit, and other values we had learned from Camp P.E. about being our Personal Best. It was fun.

On Thursday, we even went to a craft store using our weekly allowance the camp gave us, and we bought t-shirts and colored Sharpies and stencils. We spent that evening in the common room making *D&G's Basketball Camp* t-shirts for our campers as tokens. It was very relaxing work. When we were done, I thought about what tomorrow would be like. It was crazy that there was only one day left of camp.

"Hey, Gloria," I said, as I finished sewing a basketball on my last shirt, "can you believe we only have a day left?"

Gloria peered up over her final t-shirt and clapped a hand over her mouth.

"OMG, David! I'm going to really miss you," she told me. She gave me a big hug.

"Me—me too," I replied shyly. "Hey, let's just have an amazing final day tomorrow!"

On the last day, we spent the whole day having the little kids play each other, six versus six. I wanted to have it be boys against girls. True to form, however, Gloria thought that was "inappropriate" and "genderist" of me. Afterwards, we let the campers keep their t-shirts and gave each of them a huge hug goodbye. Gloria and I watched in silence as our last two campers left, Paul and Bella, a pair of siblings, ages seven and five.

"Those guys were such great kids," Gloria said in a nostalgic voice, referring to all of our campers.

"I know," I replied. "We'll have to have a reunion with them—maybe next summer." Gloria smiled and gestured toward the *Home* building.

"C'mon, Dave. My stomach's talking. I'm ready for dinner."

"Me too," I replied.

For dinner that last night, I took salad with quesadillas, along with Australian meat pie for dessert. I was going to miss all of the meal options Camp Poverty Escape gave us.

That night, after dinner, we went to an outside fire pit. There, Counselor Niasha created a big and beautiful bonfire with sparks of every color of the rainbow. As the flames from the bonfire nipped at the sky like a million colorful fireflies, Counselor Niasha stood up and gave an unforgettable speech.

"Okay, Camp P.E. members! It is time to make your experience here count for something! Try to find ways to earn money or work in your community *as soon as you can* after you return to your hometown! You have worked *hard* to learn about *resumé* writing, doing more than what is asked of you, and building your skills. Bring that grit and work as hard as you possibly can. If you do, it will bring your parents—and all of us counselors—pride, and hopefully help find a home or a ticket out of being poor! Getting to go to Camp Poverty Escape is a blessing and my hope is you will take what you learned here and not only use these skills to help your own families. I am counting on you to also use these traits to follow *your* dreams!" She paused for a moment and then said, "I believe that what you've been through makes you special. I believe you are all heroes. I believe you can use your experience both at this camp and through poverty to make a difference for others. I believe in each and every one of you!"

There was a moment of silence.

And then we all jumped to our feet and applauded as loud as a thunderstorm! Niasha looked out at us proudly, not smiling, just proud, you could tell. Soon thereafter, the counselors herded everyone back to the dorms to finish packing. I appreciated her no–nonsense encouragement of us. And I was grateful for what I'd learned that summer. At this camp, I'd learned a lot about taking care of children, cooking, writing *resumés*, responsibility, volunteer work, networking, and other important skills. And I believed it was critical that I put these skills into good use!

The next morning, Gloria and I left in an Uber to the station to catch trains back to Maryland and Ohio. When we were dropped off, Gloria and I said goodbye to each other.

"I'll call you," she told me as she gave me a hug.

"Me too!" I told her as I let go, my tears pouring. "We'll have to visit each other."

Gloria nodded. "We will," she agreed, climbing into her train car, "at our new homes!"

I liked the sound of that. I climbed up on the train to give Gloria one more hug, before I leapt back down to the platform. A lump in my throat, I turned to look up at her waving out the train window by her seat. I stood and waved, with tears streaming down my cheeks, until her train was out of sight.

I had a feeling that everything I'd learned at Camp Poverty Escape was going to be a huge help in lifting me and my family out of poverty. And it was more than that. This experience had given me a very special friendship.

In the Hole

12

Chef Kimball, Jr.

Like the train I took to the Adirondacks, the one I took back to Ohio was a little drafty and cold. But I didn't mind. At least I didn't have to walk all the way back to Wood Creek! I spent the train ride reading one of my favorite Mike Lupica books, *Heat,* before eating the hamburger and potato chips the Camp P.E. chef had packed me for lunch. I really appreciated her preparing such an awesome triple-layer burger for me, because it made it easier to not be jealous that I could not afford the great-smelling train food that everyone else was devouring. The burger reminded me of the delicious burgers my dad made, both at his former restaurant and at family barbeques! After I ate, I had a nice long nap until my train arrived in Wood Creek.

"Your stop, young man," said the kindly ticket master, patting my shoulder.

On the train platform, my family was waiting for me, all smiles. Dad wrapped me in a tight hug. Mom couldn't stop kissing me. And Julia kept jumping up and down, grabbing my arms, and squealing, "Welcome home, David!" I just accepted all the affection, snuggled with my family, and passed out the minute we arrived at the inn.

An inn may not be a real home, but having bunked there for more than two years, it felt like home. After having been away from my family for nearly two months, I never wanted to leave them again.

The very next day at breakfast, however, when Julia randomly asked, "Can Shanice, Sienna, and Polly come over?" I felt a sudden longing to see friends as well. While Justin was still in Hawaii and most of my friends were also on vacation, I knew for a fact Will was staying home for baseball. If Shanice and Sienna were home, that meant Nick and Louis probably were too.

"Mom," I asked, as I munched on my syrupy blueberry pancake, "can I go to Will's? Maybe Nick and Louis could come with their sisters here, and the three of us could walk to the Yangs' house together."

Mom nodded, smiling as a bluebird chirped outside our window. "That sounds like a good plan, sweetie," she told me, "I'll call the Lances and Albertos and tell them to bring the big sibs along too."

I gave Mom a thumbs up and wandered outside to gaze happily at the lake. It was an unusually bright blue, and the warm yellow sun shone brightly on the rippling surface of the lake. Two green-headed mallard ducks swam along together. I had a hopeful feeling that sixth grade was going to be a great year.

At around 10:00 a.m., the crowd of friends began to arrive.

"Wow!" I said, beaming as I gave Nick and Louis bro-hugs. "How've you guys been?"

"Good," Louis replied, sitting down.

"Same," Nick agreed.

"How about you, Dave? How was camp?"

"Awesome," I replied, "I made a friend, Gloria."

Nick and Louis exchanged a glance as they struggled to contain giggles.

"David's got a girlfriend?" Louis asked incredulously. He blew fake kisses in an obnoxious way.

Seriously, Louis? I thought. *What grade are you going into? Seventh or second?*

"No," I muttered flatly. "Gloria's just another best friend."

Nick gave me a thumbs up as he told Louis and me about soccer camp. "I scored at least five goals this summer," he bragged.

"Are you three still going to Will's house?" Mom asked, interrupting our conversation.

"Yeah, we were just leaving," I confirmed, as Louis hopped out of his seat.

"Be careful and watch out for cars," Mom reminded us with a wave of the vacuum wand she was eager to deploy on our floors.

"We will, Mom," I reassured her as we headed out.

Will didn't live that far away from me. In fact, he just lived a few doors down from Justin. So, only about a half hour passed before we rang the doorbell at the Yangs' house. Wearing a bright pink dress, Mrs. Yang answered the door.

"Hi, gang!" she exclaimed in her high voice as she embraced us, flipping her long black braid over her shoulder.

After asking us questions about how our moms were doing, she told us Will was in his huge bedroom. We found him there practicing baseball with one of those indoor-batting-machines. (Don't worry, the machines came with a net so Will was not destroying his walls.

Plus, Will had excellent aim.) The sound of the ball being hit was so loud that at first, he didn't hear us knocking on his door. After a few seconds of the three of us all hollering, "Will!" at the top of our lungs, he finally opened his door.

"Hey, guys, sorry."

"No, problem," I replied, patting his back.

"How's baseball been, Will?" Louis asked as we walked down Will's wooden staircase toward the dining room.

Will put on a goofy smile, and snickered. "It's been really weird without you, and you, David—and Justin. The summer league had very few players from our crew. Just me, Robby, and Max, as well as Oliver. Oh, and Otto finally decided to pick up a bat and play baseball."

"Really?" Louis asked, raising an eyebrow in surprise.

"What position does he play?"

"At the moment, he's just the back-up shortstop," replied Will.

"Though he's actually really good. If Max wasn't an incredible shortstop, there's a chance Otto would be starting."

"Has he scored any home runs yet?" Nick wanted to know, as we sat down.

"The most he's gotten is a double," Will replied, shaking his head.

Nick, Louis, Will, and I began chatting about highlights in Will's season. Mrs. Yang passed by to go into the kitchen. I listened to her foraging around for a minute or so before she walked out the front door.

"Will," she called, "I'm going to drop off your dad's snack at his workplace. The house is all yours, boys... Please don't do anything destructive!" she teased. "I'll be back soon."

"Okay, Mom!" Will called back as she left. He, Louis, Nick, and I returned to our baseball conversation. I was only half listening, however. I could still smell the snack Will's mom had made for her husband and I began to think about... making food. Lucky for me, there was a blank notebook and a pen on the kitchen table. I borrowed it and began to write as I recalled all the foods Dad had cooked at his restaurant.

Number One: Hamburgers. Dad's burgers were absolutely famous. Before his reputation was ruined because of the scandal at the restaurant, people would often go up to me in the grocery store and ask, "Aren't you the boy whose dad makes those amazing hamburgers?" And even after he lost his restaurant, Julia, and our friends, and I still always wanted Dad to grill the burgers at our birthday parties. *Hey, maybe we might even do the Camp PE Triple-Layer Burger as a special menu item!* I thought to myself, grinning.

Number Two: Apple pie. At Dad's restaurant, they didn't serve cake or ice cream for birthdays. Instead, they served the world's tastiest apple pie. One time when I was six, I got to help Dad bake a pie at his diner. He even invited me to come serve it with him! After everyone at the table had had a bite of pie, their smiles all grew big enough that you'd have thought they had won a trip to Disney World. Dad had thumped me on the back and boasted, "This gifted future chef inherited the

Kimball family talent for cooking, and he'll be running this restaurant with me when he grows up!"

Number Three: Turkey. In first and second grade, the O'Malleys came to our house for Thanksgiving. We had to stop the tradition in third grade because we couldn't afford company that year, and Justin was very disappointed. Scowling, he had told me, "I was looking forward to your dad's incredible turkey."

Number Four: Plum cakes. My great grandfather had created plum cakes—muffins with plum slices cooked in instead of blueberries. My dad brought them to Wood Creek and most of the town thought they tasted even better than the original!

I had just added *Bean & Fry* salads and *Ice Cream Sandwiches* to the list when Will peered over my shoulder.

"Hey, Dave, what are you working on?" he asked.

I took a deep breath, looked hopefully at my kind, smiling, supportive friends, and admitted what I had been thinking since I left camp. "I think," I told my friends, "that it's time for me to start my own restaurant!"

Nick began to clap his hands. "I'm first in line for those burgers!"

"Have you told your dad yet?" Louis asked curiously.

"Just you guys, just now, Louis," I replied. "I haven't told anyone else yet."

"Have you ever cooked before?" Will asked, peering at the list. His small mouth fell open and his brown eyes looked uncertain as he read. "Wow, some of these recipes look kind of advanced. Do you honestly think you can learn all of them soon enough?"

"I already know how to make apple pie and chicken salad," I replied. "And I'm sure my mom has a recipe for blueberry muffins—plum cakes are pretty much the same thing."

"What about the burgers?" Nick wanted to know.

I laughed. I'd never made burgers before, but I saw no reason why I couldn't!

"Th—thank you for the challenge, Nick," I stammered, faking confidence. "I'll see you guys in an hour!"

I went into the kitchen where the Yang's family computer was.

"Hey, Will, what's your House password?" I called.

"Shaggy," Will replied.

Like your sheepdog, I thought to myself as Shaggy actually trundled into the kitchen shaking his brown and white coat.

"Let's hope this works, Shaggy," I said as I petted his silky coat.

The password let me right in, and online I found a good burger recipe. Part of my brain was thinking: *Are you out of your mind? You are eleven and a half! There is no way you can do this!* Part of me was wondering whether I should wait for Mrs. Yang to get back so she could oversee this, just to be safe. A stronger part of me that had been nurtured a lot at Camp P.E., however, was thinking, *Come on, David! You can do it! Don't give up! Think how amazing it would be if you were able to make burgers on your own!*

I foraged in the fridge and found eggs and ground beef. Setting garlic to sizzle in an olive oil-coated frying pan, as I had seen my dad do a zillion times, I threw in some pepper. Thankfully Will's family had all of the ingredients I needed! It took all of my strength to stop myself from shaking as I flipped the garlic slices on the griddle. It hadn't occurred to me to ask if Will's mom had planned to use the ingredients for something else; I just excitedly plunged in, heedless of the consequences. I remembered to wash my hands before I started mixing the eggs into the hamburger. Adding the crisped garlic bits to the mix was easy, and forming the patties was as well. Yet it was insanely difficult not to shake when I was near the stove top.

How on earth am I going to be able to flip the patties when I can barely be near the grill without freaking out? I wondered. Then another thought hit me: *Just do it!* I placed each burger in the preheated pan and began to fiercely flip each of them with as much strength as I'd used during the free throws I had made hundreds of times in my life. I may have been acting madly, but I was still able to give each side of each burger enough time to grill fast to sear in the juices. After three minutes, they looked perfectly done, and I slowly and carefully placed each burger on a plate—all eight of them. Focusing on the task at hand—instead of on showing off—I carried the burgers into the Yang's dining room, hollering for the guys to meet me there.

Will's tongue fell out of his head.

"You—you *made* those?" He sputtered. "Dav—David you have to show Mom before we eat them. Hang on!" Will bolted back to his room and came out with his camera and shot a bunch of photos.

"What're we waiting for? Let's eat!" Louis shouted.

The burgers were rich, meaty, and delicious, and I felt *totally awesome.*

"Great job, David!" Nick told me as he gobbled down his second burger. I laughed.

"I'm not David anymore," I declared, "I am Chef Kimball, Jr.!"

The rest of the day was pretty quiet—the four of us just watched TV. At 4:30, Mrs. Alberto came and picked up Louis, Nick, and me. That night, I talked to Dad about my new business plans. When I told Dad about Nick's challenge and how successful the hamburgers had been, a tear of joy rolled down his cheek.

"It's just like I said when you helped me make that apple pie in the restaurant back when you were in first grade, son," he murmured, sniffling a little as he spoke. "I knew that just as I, your grandfather, your great-grandfather, and your great-great-grandfather had been, you're blessed with a natural skill and love for cooking."

I beamed back at him. Then, I took a deep breath and opened my mouth. It was a long moment before my words came out. "I want to start a restaurant too, Dad," I told him. "Now. *Not* wait till I grow up. I want to run it after school and on weekends."

Dad looked skeptical. "I love you, honey, but... I'm not sure it will work. In the winter, spring, and most of the summer, you're busy with basketball and baseball, not to mention your homework. Also, you're only eleven. You can't run a restaurant on your own. You need someone older to help."

"You?" I asked, grinning as I envisioned working side-by-side with my awesome, passionate, beloved father in the diner together. It would be loads of fun! While I'd been away at camp, Dad had completely stopped drinking. He was attending AA meetings almost every day and was really and truly, for the first time, *sober*. I felt positive that he was ready to get back into business!

"I don't think that's going to work, Dav-o." Dad sighed. "The last time I tried getting back to work, no one trusted me because of the mistakes I made at the old restaurant."

I protested. "Try again, Dad!"

Dad just shook his head. He was too paranoid that he had lost the community's faith forever.

"A little girl was kidnapped because I didn't pay enough attention. I wouldn't trust me either," Dad told me sadly. This was the first time Dad had verbalized to me his sense of responsibility for what had happened with the kidnapper. That was when an idea came to me.

"What if you apologize to the girl's family?"

Dad's dark eyes widened. "What did you say, David?"

"Apologize to the girl's family—the girl who was kidnapped. Might help?"

Dad hesitated. "Well, I did see in the news that after the girl was kidnapped, sometime around Halloween, my employee's wife returned the little girl to her home and confessed to the police that her husband had done it in a moment of drug-induced insanity." Then Dad added, "But how do we find the girl's family to apologize to them? Her name was never released to the newspapers because she was a minor, and the family apparently wanted to keep it quiet, probably in order to let her begin to make her way back to normal life."

"Isn't she near Julia's age?" I asked.

Dad nodded. "She's a year younger than Julia."

"Who's a year younger than me?" Julia called, getting up from the corner of the inn room where she had been playing with her toy horses.

"No one you'd know, honey," Mom interjected, glancing up from her easel. She turned to reprimand my dad, "Harry, you'll give her nightmares."

"Who?" Julia persisted, demanding with one of her horses in my face.

"A girl who was kidnapped," I replied as Julia parked herself right next to me, staring me down with a toy horse in each hand.

"Oh. He means Lila Dayal." Now Julia's other horse *spoke* for her.

Mom and Dad looked at each other nervously.

"Maybe," Dad replied to Julia's plush horse instead of confronting my little sister directly, "Horsey, can you tell us about Lila Dayal?"

Julia made her horse nod compliantly before she spoke, "Lila lives in the Southeastern part of Wood Creek and is good friends with some of Julia's friends who live there, especially Zoey."

"Very interesting," Mom coaxed, speaking directly to the horse. "And does she ride with you...?"

"Nope." There was a long silence before Julia's toy horse continued, "Last fall, at Zoey's birthday party, all of the girls in Julia's class, plus the girls in Zoey's class who Julia's class was with in kindergarten, plus a few others including Lila Dayal, were all playing *Capture the Flag*. And Zoey's dad explained the rules about taking a *prisoner*, and Lila screamed and ran inside." Julia's

177

horsey looked down and Mom petted it, coaxing it to continue. "Later on, when Julia took me to go to pee, we found Lila crying in the bathroom."

Mom, Dad, and I were stone-cold silent, hoping Julia would continue with the painful, confusing memory.

"Julia and I asked if she was okay," Julia re-enacted the scene, speaking the whole time through her little horsey, "And Lila asked us if we could keep a secret. We said yes and she told us, 'I was a prisoner once. I got kidnapped from a restaurant. And ever since I was freed, I scream if somebody says *prisoner*.'"

"So, what did, um, the three of you do?" Dad asked softly and scratched the plush horse gently under its muzzle.

"Julia and I gave Lila a hug and said that *Capture the Flag* was just a game. She smiled and we all went back outside and played."

Dad, Mom, and I exchanged glances. Their eyes were full of tears. None of us had ever told Julia why my father lost his restaurant—we all felt that she was too young to understand. But if this Lila Dayal girl had been kidnapped from a restaurant, then she had to be the same girl who was kidnapped by Dad's employee!

"Horsey," Dad said, "you may have just helped this family more than you'll ever realize. Julia, give your horse an extra scoop of oats today as our thank-you!"

Julia looked confused, then her horsey said simply, "You're welcome." My sister turned her attention to her other horses who wanted some of those oats, too.

"What if the Dayals aren't willing to see me?" Dad murmured, sinking back sullenly in his chair. "What if they won't accept my apology?" I could tell by the look on Dad's face that he was afraid.

"I know that *I'm sorry* is hard to say, Harry," Mom said gently.

"Dad, you're one of the bravest men I know. You tap-danced at the ball Ms. Maritza threw in second grade!" Dad smirked. His look of dejection fading, I looked right into Dad's eyes. "Dad, I know you can do this! I have a strong feeling that apologizing will make things better for you and our family!" I pointed at Mom who was now preparing dinner, and Julia, who was playing with her stuffed horses. "Do it for them, Dad. Do it for us!"

Dad hesitated for a brief moment before nodding. "Okay, I'll give it a try. But first, I want to acknowledge that you, David Kimball, are brilliant!"

"No less than you and Mom," I replied giving Dad a hug.

"And Julia!" yelled Julia's horsey.

Mom loved the idea of the two of us running a restaurant together and she agreed to co-sign a small bank loan together with Mrs. Brewer so that we could launch our restaurant. I also told Dad what I had learned at camp about advertising, marketing, and doing business. While we both agreed to not do any of that until after Dad's apology, we also both felt that these new skills would be beneficial.

Once school was back in session, I was very happy that Justin had finally returned home!

"How was Hawaii?" I asked him as we took our seats at the table in the front of the room for carpentry class (the only class we had together that year).

"It was good, lots of surfing and volcano exploration on Maui," Justin replied. He had gotten super tan. "I got your letters from Camp Poverty Escape."

"I got yours, too," I replied.

"So, do you still talk to this Gloria person?" Justin asked, teasing.

"Um, yes," I reddened. If Justin was going to ask me about the girls I was friends with, I might as well do the same. "What about you? Did you talk to any girls on the beach?"

"A couple," Justin replied.

"What were their names?" I asked.

"The first one was named *You-Don't-Need* and the second was named *To-Know*," Justin replied, winking and chuckling at his own stupid joke.

"C'mon, O'Malley, I told you about Gloria. You can tell me about the girls you're friends with!" I snorted, adding, "Unless of course your hotness couldn't handle the beach and decided to go on its own vacation until you got back!"

Justin groaned and swatted at me with his hand. "Fine, David, you win. Her name was Marianne. She is an indigenous Hawaiian with black hair and she's a really good hula dancer." He reached into his pocket. "You promise not to laugh?" he asked as he showed me a picture of himself and a Hawaiian girl doing the hula together.

My jaw dropped. I wanted to give Justin a "*Damn, bro!*" but of course, we were in school where that type of language is not allowed.

"Did you show him, too?" Robby grinned as he approached with Nick.

"So, what if I did?" Justin asked in annoyance. "Quit busting my chops about it, Robby!"

Robby, Nick, and I laughed.

That afternoon, my parents picked me up from school in a car I didn't recognize, a red one borrowed from a friend. Julia was already in the back seat.

"Where are we going?" I asked as I slung my heavy backpack in beside Julia's.

"We're going to Zoey's!" Julia told me excitedly.

I wondered why we'd be socializing on a school night when we both had homework. Mom explained that we were going to meet up with the Fishers—Zoey's family— who were going to introduce us to the Dayals, so that Dad could apologize. (Because the Fishers were friends with both our family and the Dayals, my parents thought having them with us would make the apology safer.)

Dad apologize? I marveled.

Meanwhile, Dad wasn't saying anything. He was looking at his hands and grinding his teeth a bit, as though he was afraid to speak. Good thing Mom was driving. I could tell he was nervous. In fact, the closer we got to the Fishers, the more Dad began to fidget. Mom actually had to coax him out of the car by gently tugging his arm. We knocked on the Fisher's wooden door and Mrs. Fisher answered.

She gave my parents a warm smile and said, "We'll be ready in a moment. Zoey's getting her shoes on."

At that moment, Zoey raced from the kitchen to hug Julia. Once Zoey's mom had checked to confirm that her shoelaces were tied, Zoey, Mrs. Fisher, Julia, Mom, Dad, and I walked to the Dayals' house two doors down. It was a very pretty shade of light blue, three stories high, and had a big yard. A couple of basset hounds were running around out front. We approached the front door. Dad's face was crimson, and he kept wiping sweat off his brow. I put an arm around him.

"Dad. C'mon. You can do this. It's going to be okay—it's going to work!"

The door was open; even so, we still rang the doorbell to be polite. A plump Indian woman with straight black hair answered the door. Behind her simple blue dress stood a tall lanky man with a black handlebar mustache and glasses. They addressed Zoey and her mom in a friendly manner before asking who we were.

"These are our friends, Charlotte and Harrison Kimball, and their son, David, and daughter, Julia," Mrs. Fisher told Mrs. Dayal.

At the mention of *Kimball*, the couple's faces fell. They exchanged an uncomfortable look.

"Aren't you the man who owned that diner where—?" He choked. His wife stood closer to him.

At this, Dad looked at the ground; he seemed to be losing his balance. I was afraid he would collapse. If that happened, the plan would be ruined!

"C'mon, Dad! You've got this!" I whispered to him, "You've made it *this* far! You can't quit now!"

At that, Dad stood straighter and, blushing, he faced the Dayals. "I should have come to you a long time ago. I am finally able to say..." Dad's hands were clasped in front of his stomach respectfully. "...I am very, *very* sorry that I wasn't paying attention when my employee kidnapped your daughter. I should have been more vigilant. I should have run a CORI check on him before I hired him. And I want you to know that if I ever run a restaurant again, I promise I will not only be extra careful about whom I hire, I will be more mindful about every single child in my establishment. I have kids of my own and—" Tears of shame and regret crept from my dad's eyes.

At this, the couple looked surprised. "Do you really mean that?" Mr. Dayal asked.

Dad nodded shyly. "Every word," he said simply.

Mr. and Mrs. Dayal exchanged a long look, like they were reading each other's minds. Mrs. Dayal nodded, almost imperceptibly, to her husband.

"You are forgiven, Mr. Kimball," said Mr. Dayal sternly.

"We appreciate this apology," Mrs. Dayal added quietly.

Dad took a deep breath before asking if the parents would allow him to apologize to Lila. There was a long pause before the couple agreed.

"Lila!" Mr. Dayal called up the stairs.

"Come down, please!" Mrs. Dayal followed.

Soon a little girl with long black hair, and holding a doll in one hand and a hairbrush in the other, bounded down the stairs. She wore purple jeans.

"Excuse us a moment," said Mrs. Dayal politely. She and Mr. Dayal took Lila aside to explain everything to her before they gestured for Dad to step inside the entryway.

Dad did as they wished and squatted down to make his formal apology to Lila Dayal.

Lila smiled at Dad and said simply, "It's okay." She even hugged Dad and gave him a squeeze. Then, turning around, she said *hi* to Zoey and Julia and Julia's horsey.

Julia stuck her plush horse out at Lila and said, "Hi, Lila!"

Lila smiled. "Can I brush your hair?" The three of them went off to play.

"Would you three like to come in for tea?" Mrs. Dayal asked graciously.

"Of course!" Mom replied. "Thank you! That is really generous of you!"

At that moment, I recalled my homework, and asked if I could go find a place to do it. Mrs. Dayal said yes and pointed to a sunny spot at the kitchen table for me to work. I dashed to the car for my backpack then back to the kitchen and pulled out my math book. There, I could smell blueberry coming from the oven and wondered if someone was baking blueberry muffins.

Minutes later, I heard clomping shoes and a deep voice as someone joined the adults.

"Here's our proud graduate!" announced Mrs. Dayal.

"Our *unemployed* graduate," remarked Mr. Dayal jovially.

"Pop, buzz off," the deep voice replied, laughing.

"Our son finished college a year early," Mrs. Dayal bragged, "he's super disciplined."

"You'll see, I'll do you proud, Pops. All that college tuition you paid won't go to waste."

Soon, the loud footsteps entered the kitchen and I glanced up in surprise at a tall man with a goatee, hair dyed yellow, and big boots. He had a big smile and a sharp nose.

"Hi!" he said in a friendly voice. "I'm guessing it's your parents I just met. Nice folks."

"Who are you?" I asked shyly.

"Jomon Dayal," he replied, smiling. "Glad to be of service."

We shook, Jomon's hand completely dwarfing mine. He then opened the oven and removed the blueberry muffins. "I love to cook," remarked Jomon. "Cooking is a lot of fun and such a great way to spend one's time, don't you think, kid?"

I nodded. "I love to cook too, and my dad does too. I'm David, by the way. Not *kid*."

Jomon smirked and nodded. "Before Lila disappeared, I used to love going to your father's restaurant with my friends. He's a great chef," Jomon added, smiling.

We talked for a few more minutes. Before we joined our parents, Jomon's muffins cooled enough that everyone could take one.

"These're terrific!" I exclaimed. "Dad, Jomon loves to cook like you and I do."

Excitedly, I exchanged a glance with Dad, who read my meaning and stepped forward. "Your dad mentioned you're job hunting." Dad smiled.

Surprised, Jomon replied, "Why?"

Wiping blueberry-drenched crumbs from his mouth, my father asked Jomon, "Hey, uh, can we chat a moment?"

Jomon nodded. "I was heading out, but—"

"He definitely has a moment!" said Mr. Dayal playfully. "He's not in a rush to be anywhere."

Mrs. Dayal glared at her husband, indicating that *that* was quite enough about *that*.

While Jomon and my dad spoke in the other room, I told Mr. and Mrs. Dayal about our list of favorite recipes.

When Dad and Jomon rejoined us, Jomon offered to type his cell number into Dad's phone.

"There, now you've got me on speed dial, if there is anything I can do for you, sir," said Jomon, handing Dad back his mobile phone.

Dad smiled, shook hands with Jomon, and turned to his parents. "We better not overstay our welcome," Dad said, eyeing the door. "It's almost time for dinner."

We said thank-you and goodbye to the Dayals and Mrs. Fisher. Dad shook hands with Mr. Dayal. Mom and Mrs. Dayal politely nodded at one another, and Julia and Lila hugged.

As we got in the car, I asked, "So, Dad, are you going to hire Jomon?"

Dad smiled at me in the rearview mirror.

"I want to learn a bit more about Jomon's cooking experience and personal life... I think he might be a great manager for the two of us, you know, and Dave, we might have you and Jomon be the face of our new restaurant!"

13

The Restaurant

The autumn of sixth grade was one of the easier seasons of my homeless days. Don't be fooled; things were still hard, but they were getting better. I was happier, I didn't cry as much as I had over the past three years, and I felt better about myself—more resilient, somehow.

With money from the bank loan, and from Mr. and Mrs. Dayal, Dad and Jomon placed a full-page advertisement in the local newspaper. The ad contained the story of how our two families reconciled, and that we were starting a new restaurant together. Dad insisted that I should be mentioned as the youngest shareholder, menu designer, *and* marketing director. In addition, the ad listed the menu offerings we anticipated serving on opening day. It included Jomon's blueberry muffins. There was also a coupon for 25% off all burgers; that helped us kick-start with quite a few customers who remembered Dad's amazing burgers and kind customer service.

While the majority of our early patrons were family friends and former customers, we still needed to persuade a *certain* group of people; namely, the folks who had refused to do business with my dad no matter where he worked because of the scandal. But when word got around that Lila's parents had forgiven my father, even these folks became more willing to give him a second chance. And as time passed, the number of second chance-givers increased more and more! It helped that everyone knew the food was delicious and fresh. After all, the quality of the food had never been the issue. And of course, the customer service was excellent!

As a result of the increase in customers, our family was finally earning a decent amount of money. After we netted out overhead costs to run the restaurant—pay rent for the space, and for food and supplies—Dad gave Jomon 40% of profits and Dad and I split the remaining 60%. It was a huge relief to know we had money coming in. Even when I felt down, it was comforting to know I could always call Justin or Gloria, or some of my other friends, for an extra boost. I usually called Gloria because of how much I missed her. She was doing a lot of babysitting and the two of us enjoyed sharing "work stories." We also talked about our families. Gloria told me about visiting her dad in prison and I told Gloria about my dad's apology, which she thought was amazing.

The number of customers at our new restaurant kept increasing. Folks knew that they were getting their money's worth, that was for sure. In fact, once after I served a burger that I had made, to a boy around Julia's age, the kid told me that I should give *his* dad lessons.

"Put that in your *resumé* for college," chuckled Dad.

It was cool hanging out with Jomon while we cooked and after we finished work. It felt awesome to have an older friend. Sure, Louis, Sam, and Will were all a year older than me, but because it was just one year, it didn't feel that significant. The fact that a college graduate was willing to be partners and friends with me—a sixth grader—felt amazing. It was a chance for me to learn a lot from a guy who felt like my big brother.

After work, Jomon sometimes came back to the inn with Dad and me, and other times I would go to his house. We played *War*, *Uno*, *Go Fish*, and other card games. Once in a while, Jomon took me to a great pizzeria in Northern Wood Creek, in part to scout their delicious pizza recipe, and to play video games, and talk about whatever was going on in our minds.

We weren't always in sync, however. We argued once in October. He didn't like the idea of baking an entire pie for a customer's birthday, rather than a cupcake or ice cream cone, which would be more cost-effective for us.

"What's wrong with a simple blueberry muffin?" he challenged me.

We debated which was better, insulting each other in the process. Ultimately, I explained to him that pie was a Kimball family tradition: we'd always served apple pie at our family birthday parties. In the end, Jomon understood and respected our family's tradition.

Also, as close as we were, Jomon and I didn't have that much in common. Jomon was obsessed with horror movies. (Much like my roommate from Camp P.E.— except Jomon was a lot less insane!) Personally, I preferred the *Justice League* type of genre. Jomon was kind of into watching sports—badminton was the only sport he actually played. And as you know, baseball and basketball were my *life* when I was growing up. Our cooking interests were not always eye to eye either. Jomon wanted to cook more spicy Indian food, while Dad and I were more into standard American fare. Even so, Jomon and I were still very tight. We shared a lot of personal things with each other, and neither of us would ever betray our friendship. Nor would either of us ever bamboozle the other into taking less money than each of us had earned.

One Saturday night in November, I went to a trivia competition with him, his girlfriend, Daniella, and Daniella's sister, Shelby, who was my age. Unfortunately, Shelby was way too competitive and kept passing me notes with the answers in an attempt to trick me into losing. For a while she gave me the wrong answers, then for a while she gave me the right ones, and finally, she gave me a mix of both. Feeling annoyed, I eventually just started throwing the notes she passed me right where they belonged—in the trash. Jomon was sympathetic, as he said, "I don't want to disrespect my girl by talking smack about her sis." Peacemaker that Jomon was, instead, he just apologized to me, saying that Shelby gets carried away and can at times be "a little too competitive." *I'll say!*

Meanwhile, our restaurant, *Kimball & Dayal's Diner,* continued to do well. We made weekly bank deposits with the money from the restaurant. Of course, the bank manager knew about the restaurant— sometimes he even brought his family! And he was impressed with how much money we made. "You gentlemen are doing very good work to be able to make this much a week," he remarked when we handed him a larger-than-usual wad of cash to deposit. "Keep it up!"

I was also very good at saving. It was exciting to see my savings getting higher and higher. When you are homeless, something in your gut helps you make a small amount of money last for a long time. By December, I had earned enough money that I was able to buy round trip tickets for a cheap train to Maryland so I could visit Gloria for her birthday! Not only that, Jomon and I had enough money in our restaurant budget that we were able to buy a couple of mismatched tables from a yard sale for the restaurant. To give you a visual on how happy my parents were when I handed them $500 on Christmas day, I'll say that Mom could not stop dancing around the inn and Dad invited Jomon and Daniella over for Christmas dinner.

That night, Dad gushed to Jomon about how grateful he was to him for working with us, "You are a fine young man, and a great influence on our son. My family and I could not appreciate you more!" Dad proclaimed, wiping away tears.

On New Year's Day, the moment we unlocked the doors of the restaurant, about three dozen people came in shouting "Happy New Year!" at the top of their lungs. They blew those kazoos you blow at birthday parties, and everyone got comfortable. When there wasn't enough room for everyone, a line formed out the door, and one person even went home and came back to donate an expensive-looking bench to the restaurant which Jomon, Dad, and I accepted gratefully. It was long and topped with copper—long enough to fit seven people! I was delighted. I recalled when the restaurant had first opened, and we barely had ten customers a night. Now we were serving an average of forty every evening! If that doesn't demonstrate how far someone can advance in four months, I don't know what does.

"Maybe we should hire a waiter," Dad suggested, "so people don't have to wait so long for their food."

Jomon frowned. "I don't know, Harry. That might be kind of expensive. Are you sure we shouldn't just get a serve-yourself bar? What do you think, David?"

I thought about that. Neither were bad ideas. But I liked Jomon's idea better. To earn money for my family quickly, it was better to work with just Jomon to keep a buffet filled with fresh foods; and the three of us would take turns serving people at their tables when necessary. Overall, I felt that things were definitely heading in the right direction. And I could almost taste the feeling of having a place to call home again!

14

Rising

From January to May, and through the second half of that first year, the restaurant took in an insane amount of money. Granted, we had to deduct overhead costs before we netted a profit. Then we had to deduct state and federal corporate taxes before we paid ourselves, and we also had to deduct taxes from the wages we got as *individuals*—although I didn't have to because I was a kid and my parents just stuck it in a 529 college savings account for me. I was learning *a lot* about money! Still, having been broke for years, it was a huge relief.

One day sometime in April, while Jomon was managing the restaurant and I was at school, Dad went to the Men's Warehouse and bought himself a suit. He needed it for interviews for a better job, in order to earn more money. Half the week, he went to interview lunches in a suit and tie, and the other half, he worked at the restaurant with Jomon and me. On days when he suited up, he usually came home looking discouraged.

Then, one day during the first week of May, he came home looking like Christmas had arrived seven months early!

"What happened, Dad?" I asked, surprised, as I took in my dad's toothy beam.

"Tell you later, Dav-O," replied Dad mysteriously, and he then snuggled up to my mother and whispered, "Charlotte, won't you join me outside? We need to talk!"

Mom raised her eyebrows, nodded, and followed Dad.

I tried hard to listen in, but I could only catch a couple of words. I caught the phrases "The Raven," as well as "a job for you as well," and finally, "Badger Avenue." I wondered what all of those things meant.

Days later, something equally strange happened. My parents called a family meeting.

"Kids, we need you to stay with friends over Memorial Day weekend. Jomon will be managing the restaurant, don't worry. Which would you prefer, sticking together and going to either the Lances' or the Allens', or staying with your besties?"

I didn't need to think twice. How ironic was it that earlier that day, Robby had told Justin that he couldn't go with him on his Jersey Shore trip this year! I doubted the O'Malleys would mind taking me along instead.

"Justin," I said immediately.

My parents nodded and Mom told me she'd call Mrs. O'Malley that night.

Shortly thereafter, Jomon pulled Dad and me aside at the restaurant when I arrived from baseball practice.

"Big news!" he exclaimed. "Daniella and I are getting married this summer and after our wedding, we're moving to Oregon! So I'm sorry to say, I don't think I'll be able to keep working at the restaurant."

"Er—congratulations," I said trying to ignore the sadness and panic that welled up in my brain, heart, and gut. Jomon had become like family to me over the past year! I would miss him. Badly.

Dad just shrugged. "I'm thinking of selling the restaurant anyway," he told us.

O—kay! I thought. That was news to me! "What? Why?" I asked in surprise. Dad grinned at me in a way I found a little obnoxious. Not only had I *not* been consulted about selling the restaurant, *now*, after we'd shared our hardest times, it seemed Dad wasn't being forthcoming with information that I needed to know.

"You'll see," he told me.

At that point, I snapped, "You don't get to sell *our* restaurant—not to mention, a restaurant that was *my* idea—and not discuss it with me ahead of time!"

"I'm sorry you are upset about it, David." Dad turned bright red. "I can only hope that by the end of the month, my reasoning will be clear."

Given the look of joy on Dad's face, I nodded. Although still feeling angry and betrayed, *and* underappreciated, I decided to suck it up and be mature. I trusted that my father must have a reason that served our family. I got it that sometimes there's stuff parents simply cannot share with their children.

A couple of weeks later, I went with Justin to the Jersey shore. We had a great time. Justin and his family slept in hammocks during the trip and thankfully, there was an extra one for me. It was very peaceful to sway in the hammock at night and look at the moon and listen to evening creatures, like crickets and owls, chirp and hoot. I loved going to sleep feeling the swift, warm wind on my face, while I looked at the beautiful white moon, and listened to the crab's shuffle and click on the beach, and the seagulls' squawk. Justin and I would chat about MLB games we had watched on TV, about our friends, and other stuff, just as we did during sleepovers back in Ohio. In fact, to prevent us from talking too much, Mr. and Mrs. O'Malley eventually made Justin's brother, Eric, a sophomore in high school at the time, sleep in a hammock between us.

For breakfast, Justin and I devoured waffles with globs of butter and tons of maple syrup, before we walked along the beach into town. One morning, we hung around the Museum of Native American Culture and learned about the indigenous peoples who had lived in what is now New Jersey. I enjoyed examining each exhibit. We were impressed to learn that the Native Americans invented lacrosse, and sad to learn about them being abused and evicted from their homeland. I thought a lot about how they, too, had been forced from their homes to become homeless.

Around lunchtime, after our stomachs started grumbling, Justin and I went to a nearby diner and ate fries, hot dogs, and salad for lunch—which we could now *both* pay for. It felt liberating to no longer need Justin to pay for everything. We talked about baseball and our families and took selfies together. My parents had shocked me a week before I had left for the shore by giving me an iPhone. It was a cheap iPhone 6, with a plain, kind of ugly yellow case. I didn't care; it was enough to finally have a phone. Justin, meanwhile, had had a phone since September.

After lunch, the two of us headed back to the beach to swim and surf. (Justin's dad had taught us how to surf, having surfed all over the world himself, "from

Maui in Hawaii to Tamraght in Morocco," he liked to boast.) Once we were done surfing, we showered, grabbed snacks, napped in the hammock, and read comic books before going to eat dinner with Justin's parents and Eric. On Saturday night, I surprised the O'Malleys by making them pepperoni pizza while Justin was reading comic books. They loved the pizza, and after dinner, we all went to the local movie theater. Afterwards, we clambered back into those awesome hammocks and swung back and forth until we fell asleep.

On Sunday at lunchtime, as Justin and I munched our French fries, I felt a little funny. I wasn't sick, I could tell that, but something felt strange. If anything, it was the opposite of sick. My heart seemed to be beating very, very quickly and I had an odd sense of being happier than usual. "Justin," I asked as I finished swallowing a handful of fries, "does something feel off to you? In a good way."

Justin looked at me in confusion. "No, David, life is perfect. Why?" he asked. I shrugged.

"I'm just getting this odd vibe that something wonderful is happening. Or about to happen." I thought about it for a moment.

"Dreaming of your lover?" Justin asked teasingly. I shook my head.

"I don't have a lover," I told him.

"What about that girl from your camp?" Justin asked, winking at me as he sipped his soda.

I was tempted to throw a fry at him.

"Gloria and I are just friends, Justin!" At that moment, it occurred to me that maybe I was about to see Gloria and *that* was what the odd feeling was. "Hey, maybe we are about to run into her? I always wanted you guys to meet."

"I thought you said that your friend was homeless too! How could she afford to go to the Jersey Shore?"

"You never know. She could have gone with a friend. Look at us," I pointed out, as I stuffed a fry into my mouth. I shook my head. "It's probably unlikely though."

"Maybe a sports scout is about to approach you, one who has watched you play baseball and basketball, and he's going to invite you to go to some fancy private school on a sports scholarship," Justin suggested.

Smirking, I spat out my fry after nearly choking on it. "First of all, there is no way a scout could watch me play baseball and offer me a scholarship for that without offering you one too! And second of all, that is just as likely as Gloria coming here! I mean, how would the scout even know we were in New Jersey?"

"The scout could always approach you when you're back in Ohio," Justin told me as he finished his fries and handed me his share of the tab. "C'mon, bro, pay up and let's go grab our boards!"

I nodded as I paid our waiter, and then we raced each other back to get our surfboards and headed to the beach.

As we got out into deeper water, I got distracted by the waves crashing and I lost sight of Justin. Thankfully, it only took me twenty seconds to spot him. Then, I nearly fell off my surfboard in shock when I saw him talking to three giggly girls who looked like supermodels. Naturally, I surfed over to where they were balancing on their boards.

"Hey, Flirtface!" I hollered, laughing. The girls giggled. "New friends, Justin?"

He introduced the girls as Katie, Ariana, and Rachel, who smiled at me cheerfully and began to talk to us about baseball and cheerleading. Justin told me that he'd known these girls for a few years. They saw each other during almost every Memorial Day vacation at the shore.

"Is Robby friends with them too?" I asked.

"Yes," Justin replied.

"Where *is* Robby?" Ariana asked as the wind blew about her black hair.

"He went to the mountains with his mom and dad," Justin replied. "They wanted their own vacation with him this year. So, I brought my other best friend instead, David." He added, "You want to know a really cool thing about David? He started a restaurant with his dad this year, and he is quite the cook. Last night he made a whole pepperoni pizza all by himself and it tasted like it was from Italy!"

"Wow, that's impressive," said Katie. "Great job, David!"

"Thanks," I replied, blushing a little.

"I could use a cooking lesson. Do you know how to make waffles?" Rachel asked.

I thought about it. I'd helped Dad make waffles a few times. "Yes, I've made waffles be—*aghhhhh!*" I had gotten so super-focused on our conversation that I had forgotten to watch out for my balance, and I fell off my board as a giant wave swept me up and plunged me under. I went tumbling into the surf as it crashed, and I felt the pull of the riptide pulling me further under the water and out to sea—*fast*. I held my breath and the world seemed to spin in circles as I tried to figure out in which direction the shore lay. When I realized that the shore was in approximately the same direction that the reverse current flowed, I allowed the ocean to pull me toward the beach and then back out, toward the beach and then back out. Thank God I was always a strong swimmer! As I was being dragged out to sea, I somehow managed to swim to the surface, and was very thankful to get a lungful of air. I started to swim sideways—not toward the beach, as you might expect—but *across* the current, parallel to the beach. The riptide still pulled at me, so as I swam across the current, I was able to gradually angle toward shore. (Never, *ever* swim directly *against* the current. That will only exhaust you and potentially get you sucked out to sea where you might drown.) Trying to stay calm, I continued to swim slowly but surely, sometimes switching to the backstroke as a kind of rest. Finally, as I was nearing shore, a new wave came thundering in and heaved my exhausted form onto the beach. Coincidentally, I landed alongside my surfboard, and I lay on the shore panting with my eyes shut as the sun beat down on me. When I opened them, Justin and the girls were staring down with concern.

"We thought we lost you!" exclaimed Ariana, a frightened look on her face.

"You okay, David?" Justin asked as he put a hand on my shoulder.

"Yeah," I breathed, relieved.

The three girls gushed about how brave I was and how cool it was that I knew how to swim out of a riptide.

"You seem like a pretty talented kid," Ariana told me. "You can cook, you can swim..."

"David's an impressive athlete, too," Justin added, winking at me goofily.

I just laughed. The compliments felt good. Still, I knew getting their praise was nothing compared to whatever had given me that excited vibe earlier. As I sat on the sand, I took several long deep breaths before telling Justin I wanted to go back to the beach house to rest a bit. We said goodbye to the girls and headed back.

The weird happy vibe wouldn't leave me alone all night—it was like my instinct was on red alert. And it stayed with me as I went home with Justin and his family on Monday after lunch. When we got back to Wood Creek, Mrs. O'Malley drove right past both Justin's house and the inn. That was odd.

"Um, Mrs. O'Malley," I said, confused, "you missed the inn."

She and Mr. O'Malley shared a good chuckle. "We're not dropping you off at the inn, honey," Mrs. O'Malley told me.

"We passed home too, Mom," Justin said as we drove on past the school.

"David's not getting picked up at our house either," Justin's mom replied. "In fact, David's not getting picked up at *all*."

"He's meeting his parents *here*," said Mr. O'Malley with a smile as the car turned down Badger Avenue.

Where? I wondered.

Justin's mom drove a couple doors down before parking in the driveway of a small blue house. There was a bright lush garden in the front and a tree full of magnolias.

"Why are we here?" Justin asked, exchanging a puzzled glance with me. "We don't know anyone who lives in this house."

"Yes, we do," Mr. O'Malley replied, "In fact, someone who lives in this house is in our car."

I felt my jaw drop as I connected the dots. *Could it have happened? Has my dream come true? Was my long nightmare of being without a real home finally over?* There was only one way to find out! I raced to the door and rang the doorbell. Mom answered and gave me a hug.

"Welcome home, David!" *Yes!*

Unable to control my feelings, I burst into tears of joy and started jumping up and down. "Does Dad have a job with real pay again?" I asked, sniffling.

"We both do," Mom told me as we went to grab my stuff from the O'Malley's car. "Do you know about *The Raven*—that fancy restaurant in Northern Wood Creek?"

I nodded. "What about it?"

"Well, they wanted to make their restaurant more affordable and less fancy—and they also heard about some of your father's creative food mixes such as our plum cakes and his Bean & Fry salad. They offered to hire Dad as their new *sous chef*, complete with full medical benefits, 401K, vacation time, and even a share in the business!" Mom bit back a grin. "And David, Dad sneaked a few of my paintings with him to his interview and the people who run *The Raven* loved them and they offered to give me a job, too! They commissioned me to produce paintings for their restaurant, to hang on the walls. I get to choose a new theme every month!"

I laughed. Maybe Mom hadn't been ready to show her talent herself, still, she'd gotten a job as an artist with Dad showing off her work! "I told you your paintings were good enough for you to make a living out of them, Mom!" I blurted out.

"Oh hush," Mom muttered, looking at the ground and turning red!

I turned to Justin. "I finally have a home again, Justin," I whispered.

"Awesome, David!"

Justin hugged me, and we went inside together to explore. It felt particularly good doing it together because the truth is, I never would have survived being homeless without Justin.

It was a small house with two floors. On the ground floor, there was a kitchen, a living room, a bathroom and one bedroom, and two bedrooms upstairs. I opted for the bedroom downstairs, while my parents and Julia chose to be upstairs. Compared to our original home, this was small; there was no question about that. It was, however, a *real home*, and I had my *own room*. After living in my car for four months and a room at that inn for three years, I would take this house any day!

I called all my friends to tell them my happy news: Gloria, Nick, Sam, Louis, Will, Max, Robby, Otto, Eliot, Jomon, and even Pete Zimmerman, my old basketball teammate who moved to Florida a couple of years before. They were all really happy for me, and I was grateful for *them*. They were a huge reason why I had survived being *in the hole*. They made my life easier during the hardest times—whether by letting me hang out at their homes with them or by playing sports with me—they brought light into a time of real darkness in my life.

I'd only been home briefly—I'll never forget how happy I was to finally have a place to call home—when Dad knocked on my bedroom door.

"Dav-O, do you want to help me make dinner?" he asked. "I think having some Chef-Kimball-Jr.-burgers would be the perfect way to celebrate this occasion!" I nodded eagerly.

As I grilled the hamburgers, I thought about the crazy four years that had gone by. I hadn't had a home for three and a half of them. I had learned lessons I would never forget. I had been through enough rough stuff to last a lifetime. Yet I'd survived. We'd survived *together*. As I set out the ketchup and mustard with the plates and flatware, I overheard Julia in the next room.

"Mom, can Ella and I have a sleepover this weekend?"

I grinned to myself. At least I would be able to escape now whenever Ella, Shanice, Sienna, or any of Julia's other buddies came over for sleepovers. However, while I still cherished my privacy, I didn't mind my sister or her friends as much anymore. From the twenty-six girls who had given Julia regular visits when she was in the hospital, to Lila Dayal, I was grateful to Julia's friends for helping her through such an awful ordeal. I was also grateful for Mom and Dad's friends—not the pigs Dad went to the bar with, mind you!—but the *real* friends who helped us during the past four years. One thing was for sure, the journey wouldn't have been nearly as survivable without friends—for any of us.

The journey wouldn't have been possible without each other, either.

My parents told me over dinner that my dad had sold the old restaurant's business license and permit to a local couple he interviewed, on the condition that they choose a different name for it. (They renamed it "The Public's Feast.") Like us, the couple was very fond of cooking. My parents also said that we got a good five thousand dollars from the buyers, which Mom and Dad were able to use as part of the down payment for the new house. Having been homeless, we were very careful about money.

That night, I listened to Mom talk on the phone with a friend from church and felt extra grateful to her for staying strong for the family during those hard years. I wondered what would have happened to my family if I had had a different mother. My family would have almost certainly had a harder time staying hopeful and positive, that is for sure. My father would definitely have fallen apart completely, and Julia and I would probably have been placed in foster care and maybe even been separated from one another.

Julia had a riding show a couple of weeks after we arrived at our new home. As I tagged along to watch, I noticed how alive and happy she looked. I recalled that awful month when she was trapped in a coma and barely alive. *What if Julia had died?* I pushed that horrible thought out of my mind. After all, not only had she survived, she was perfectly healthy again! As she trotted her horse around the track, she looked completely different from the girl with the bandaged head lying unconscious in the hospital, a year and a half earlier. *Amazing.*

Toward the end of that summer, my dad insisted on throwing a party to celebrate the fact that our family had a home again. The rest of us thought that was a great idea! Dad and I made a cherry pie together in our new kitchen, and my family invited almost everyone we knew. It was fun. We played games, sang, chatted, and ate great food. A pair of Dad's friends from Alcoholics Anonymous, who happened to be mischievous types, took out the garden hose and squirted kids playing in the front yard. The adults enjoyed making the kids scream and run desperately out of the cold spray. I avoided getting drenched by staying near the food table.

One not very great habit of mine that I must admit to here is that whenever I'm near a stack of hot dogs, I cannot stop eating them. It took a lot of willpower to devour just two of them while I was hiding by the food during the drenching. Once it was safe to wander around the yard without getting soaked, I grabbed four more hot dogs and a plate, and dashed off to join Gloria in the sunshine by the porch. (I'd bought her round-trip tickets so she could come from Maryland for the celebration.) When I joined her, Gloria was completely soaked from the hose attack, and smiling happily.

"That was funny," she said, her infectious smile made me laugh.

I showed her the plate of hot dogs I had swiped. "Want one?" I offered.

"Don't mind if I do!" She replied, and snapped up one of the hot dogs. "Your house is beautiful, David. I'm really happy for you!"

"Thanks," I replied, gazing happily at its blue exterior, and recalling how judgmental about 'the perfect house' I had been when I was six and seven-years-old. Back then, I would never have tolerated living in a house without a video game console, fewer than three floors, and no basketball hoop. After all I'd been through, now, *this* house was perfect, because it was a real home. I thought again of the many people who had helped me endure and ultimately clobber poverty and homelessness: my family, Justin, Gloria, and the rest of my friends, and Jomon Dayal. They had given me hope and inspired my hard-work and determination.

I looked up to the sky where I imagined God was, and whispered in a tight voice, "Thank you."

"David, are you talking to yourself?" Gloria seemed concerned.

I considered not expressing my emotions, then decided, *Nah.* "Gloria," I said quietly, knowing she'd know exactly what I meant, "I'm just really grateful that I escaped *the hole.*" Then I remembered she was still homeless. How could I have been so insensitive? I quickly added, "It's gonna happen to you too, Gloria! You and your family will make it out too."

Gloria smiled. "Thanks, David... seeing you rise has actually inspired me to hope." I gave her a hug, and we went back to our hot dogs.

As the months went by, and I watched Dad come home from work each day all smiles and looking healthy in his *sous chef* uniform, I thought about how different he was from when he was trapped by alcohol. He still needed to lose some weight and he would never be totally free from addiction—he was learning to manage it with his meetings and Alcoholics Anonymous friends. But that didn't change how *much* he had overcome, and how *far* he had come. Plus, he was my cooking inspiration, even after he had lost his job. Without him, I might never have taken an interest in cooking and found the ladder up and out of homelessness! Together, my family and I had made it—out of *the hole*.

Epilogue

The period my family and I spent *in the hole* was possibly the hardest and yet most meaningful stretch of my life. After we found our new home, life got better for my family, but I never forgot the terrible ache of having been *in the hole* of poverty and homelessness. After everything I had experienced, I wanted to help others facing similar struggles. I just didn't know yet in *what* way. That is, until the year 2020. I was a freshman in college at Ohio State when Coronavirus exploded in the United States—and the world. During this very difficult phase in our history, the worst hit by the sickness were the homeless and impoverished who were already struggling mightily long before the Coronavirus. Things got even worse during the pandemic; most homeless people had nowhere to go, especially those who lived on the streets.

At the time, from the safety of self-quarantine with my family, I thought of what Julia had faced almost a decade earlier, and how desperate my family had been to get her the help she needed. The beginning stages of the pandemic were a pivotal time in my life, for it was during this period that I decided to commit my life to helping the homeless in any way I could. I felt compelled to talk to Gloria about my decision. At this point, thrillingly, she had her father back after a judge ordered a new trial that resulted in her dad's acquittal. She also had a home again. As fate would have it, Gloria was raising money for the homeless from her home in Maryland. We decided to create a crowdfunding campaign together so that people could donate money for supplies to support the homeless. We called the fund *Kimball & Zayes Fund for the Homeless.*

As the pandemic raged on, I learned that increased homelessness would continue to be a massive problem long after the pandemic was over. The economy was very hard hit during the shut-down, so the numbers of homeless and destitute people increased exponentially. In 2020, there were 580,466 homeless people in the United States. When I first heard this statistic, I thought about how much it had meant to my family when people tried to help us. I knew providing aid would mean a lot to those who were suffering.

After the Coronavirus crisis subsided somewhat, I returned to college and started taking courses in public policy and social justice. I travelled weekends and holidays around the state of Ohio petitioning towns to start homeless shelters and inns with lower rates. I wrote to businesses encouraging them to hire more homeless people, especially those who were stable and ready to go back to work. For those who were struggling with alcohol and drugs, as my dad had done, I raised money for their treatment, or to be transported to Alcoholics Anonymous or other "12-step" programs. Sometimes, especially during the summer, I also visited states that border Ohio, such as Kentucky and Indiana. I continued to collect sleeping bags, food, toiletries, clothes, and other necessities to donate to families who needed them. I even got interviewed one time on our local TV news and I made an inspirational speech encouraging others to do what they could to help those in need.

Then, just months before my college graduation, I met a beautiful woman named Sarah. Amazingly, when she was fifteen, her dad had lost his job and her family was kicked out of their house eight months later. In other words, she had been homeless too!

We dated briefly and married within the year. (Sometimes, you just know!) For the wedding, Sarah came up with an inspired, albeit crazy, idea: We donated to the homeless a portion of the money we received from our wedding. I loved the way Sarah's mind worked. Then I came up with an equally crazy idea—we had a small wedding ceremony at the inn where my family and I had lived. We held the reception at a nearby dance hall so that everyone could attend.

Sarah and I chose humble clothes for the wedding: my dad's old suit for me (tailored to my height!), and a simple white dress for Sarah—no veil. We wanted to show people where we had come from. We didn't care if people belittled us for wearing modest clothes at our wedding. We were representing our backgrounds and we loved it, and so did our parents and siblings.

Sarah went on to become an attorney, and I got a job as an English teacher at a middle school where I coached the sports I had loved as a boy. We had two sons, Alex and Ryan. We told our children about our experiences. We taught them to donate money and to care more about people than things. At every holiday, we donated to those in need so they could have a better holiday, too.

There's one more story I want to share with you... Shortly after he started fifth grade, my younger son, Ryan, came home from school very upset.

"Hey, buddy, what's wrong?" I asked.

"My school is raising money for a swimming pool," he said, annoyed.

"A pool?" I asked, confused. Why would Ryan be upset about that? He loved to swim!

"We already have an Olympic-size pool at our school," Ryan explained. "I think it's a waste of money. Why should we get a second pool when there are people starving? They need the money more than we need another pool!"

Sarah and I exchanged a look of pride and we both high-fived Ryan.

"Baby, we could not agree more," Sarah told Ryan as she typed on her computer. She printed out three pieces of paper with the heading, *No Extra Pools Until There is Enough Food for Everyone*. "You know what we are going to do, Ryan? We are going to petition the school to do the right thing."

"*All-right!*" I exclaimed and kissed her. As teaching had taken center stage, I'd had less time for activism. I missed the days of petitioning to make things better for the homeless. And Sarah knew it.

Our elder son, Alex helped with the petition, too. After a week, we brought the signed petition to the principal of our boys' elementary school. After he looked it over, he nodded. He showed the petition to the student government and they agreed. The second pool idea was abandoned. Instead, it was replaced with the idea of opening a soup kitchen staffed by students and volunteer parents.

On Opening Day, I was asked to make a speech. Just as we had with our wedding, I wore plain clothes—just a blue button down and nice trousers. (I even considered not wearing a tie, but Sarah insisted I wear one.)

"Thank you for coming today," I told the crowd of students and parents, and some homeless folks who had come for a free meal. "To those of you who are unsheltered, I want to let you know I've been where you are, and I know that it is rough, but you cannot give up. Keep believing and hoping and working hard. And as a result, you will eventually be raised out of *the hole* of poverty. Another thing I want you to remember, you are not alone. There are many conscious minds in America who recognize that it is our job as decent human beings to help our fellow citizens in any way we can, and that includes the homeless. We must accept that it is *our responsibility* to help you all out, to provide you with food and shelter, to make clothes donations, and, most importantly, to create opportunities for you to gain skills to help you become *self-sustaining*. We know that we *must* help and *will* help in any way we can. We must ask business owners to hire you and work with city planners and developers to invest in the building of affordable housing. It is up to us, all of America's children as a whole, sheltered and unsheltered, to unite, work together, and make sure everyone is released from *the hole* of poverty and homelessness! We are in this together for the long haul."

And we really are.

Acknowledgements

I'd like to thank...

My mother, Susan Levin, for finding me great editors and for giving *In the Hole* some edits herself;

My father, Sean Levin, also for helping to edit *In the Hole*;

My brother, Jake Levin, for all of his support and advice;

My Development-Editor and Literary Agent, Ghia Truesdale, who, from the start, believed in me and in the story and message of *In the Hole*, and who saw things in me that I couldn't necessarily see in myself; also Ania Hearn, Ghia's Editorial Assistant, for her contributions;

My Publishers, Gene Rowley and Kyle Hannah at Jumpmaster Press,™ for taking me and my books under their wing;

Kathryn Hall, my other editor, who gave the book so much consideration and thought and helped make the book all it could be;

All of the experts on homelessness who patiently shared their experience, wisdom, and understanding with me, and who helped me to understand the true nature of the crisis much more deeply: Maria Foscarinis, Founder of the National Homelessness Law Center and Antonia Fasanelli, Executive Director there; Michael Nolan, Founder of Just Love More; Noelani Reyes of ShelterSuit-NYC; David Horst-Loy, who shared his experience giving pastoral counseling to the homeless in Connecticut; Cassie Roach of Santa Barbara's Safe Parking Program; Kate Duggan, Executive Director of

Family Promise of Bergen County; and Kirsten Corley of Covenant House, New Jersey;

My grandfather, Professor Herman Schwartz, for connecting me to the National Homelessness Law Center—where he was Chairman of the Board for many years;

My grandmother, Mary C. Schwartz, who reads my stories with me and gives me her honest input;

My Grandma Ro, who always lets me know she cares;

Marsha Mello, who donated her beautiful illustration of *home* for the Dedication page;

Meryl Moss and Jim Alkon at Booktrib;

My English teachers from 8th grade through 10th grade with whom I've gone over the book and who gave good edits, especially Vani Apanosian;

Zach Martin of New HDMedia, who helps me to believe in my gifts;

All my advance readers, who gave their time and input.

Resource List

Resources for Unsheltered People and Families, and also for Good Souls who Want to Learn More About the Homelessness Crisis

Covenant House provides housing and supportive services to youth facing homelessness. They help young people transform their lives and put them on a path to independence.

Covenant House has branches all over the country, including in Washington, DC, New York City, and New Jersey. (https://www.covenanthouse.org)

Just Love More in Atlanta, GA, addiction services for unsheltered individuals. *You need help, not judgement.* Addiction affects many of us. Stigma makes it even harder to ask for help when we need it. Just Love More offers support without judgment. No one knows what you need better than you, so we help you make your own choices about recovery, then support you in creating a plan to get there. (https://www.justlovemore.org)

The Substance Abuse and Mental Health Services Administration (SAMHSA) Hotline. SAMHSA's National Helpline, 1-800-662-HELP (4357), (also known as the Treatment Referral Routing Service) or TTY: 1-800-487-4889 is a confidential, free, 24-hour-a-day, 365-day-a-year, information service, in English and Spanish, for individuals and family members facing mental and/or substance use disorders. This service provides referrals to local treatment facilities, support groups (like A.A.), and community-based organizations.

Alateen Groups. Alateen is a place for teens affected by the alcoholism of family members and/or friends. At Alateen, members come together to share experiences, strength, and hope with each other to find effective ways to cope with problems, discuss difficulties and encourage one another, and to help each other understand the principles of the Al-Anon program through the use of the Twelve Steps and Alateen's Twelve Traditions. (https://al-anon.org/newcomers/teen-corner-alateen)

New Beginnings Counseling Center (NBCC) in Santa Barbara, CA, is committed to strengthening our community. Our mission is to provide our clients with the ability to lead healthy and productive lives through our Counseling Clinic, our Life Skills Parenting and Education Program, our Safe Parking and Rapid Re-Housing Program and our Supportive Services for Veterans Families Program. (https://sbnbcc.org)

The National Homelessness Law Center, the only national organization dedicated solely to using the power of the law to end and prevent homelessness and to protect the rights of people experiencing homelessness. (https://nlchp.org)

Family Promise of Bergen County. Our Promise is to empower homeless working families to become self-sufficient. Programs range from providing temporary

shelter, to ongoing support as families transition to permanent housing.
(https://www.bergenfamilypromise.org)

Sheltersuit NYC provides immediate shelter to the homeless, while using upcycled material and providing jobs. Since 2014, Sheltersuit has designed and manufactured emergency disaster relief, multifunctional products that provide immediate shelter to people experiencing homelessness.
(http://www.sheltersuit.com)

Questions for Book Club Study of *In the Hole*

1. What does the phrase *"in the hole"* mean to you? Why do you think the author chose it for the title?

2. Throughout the story, the author places enormous emphasis on the support David receives from his friends and family. How have your family and friends supported you as you went through hard times in your life?

3. David is crushed when he loses his PlayStation, one of his most prized possessions. What possessions of your own are most meaningful to you, and how would you feel if you had to give it up for the sake of your family?

4. Throughout the book, whenever David has a conflict, he solves it by using his ingenuity, such as when he sells found objects to raise some cash for his family. Have there been situations in your life where you have been forced to use your own creativity to resolve a conflict? What were the circumstances and how did things turn out?

5. Which character in the story did you most relate to, and why?

6. In the book, at first David chooses not to share the details of his situation with the majority of his friends. What would you do in his position? Have you ever had a secret you were afraid to share with your friends? What was it?

7. In the story, David has five people with whom he primarily interacts. His mom, his dad, Julia, Justin, and Gloria. In what ways are these relationships similar? In what ways are they different? For example, how is David's friendship with Justin similar to his friendship with Gloria? How are the relationships different?

8. Respectively, how would you compare David's relationships with his parents?

9. One thing that helps David and Gloria connect is the fact that they are both *homeless*. Have any of your conflicts and similar experiences helped you to bond with your friends? How so?

10. As David matures through the course of the book, he finds opportunities to help both of his parents with some of their challenges. Can you think of some examples of times when David helps his mom? His dad? Do you sometimes try to help out your parents, when they seem to need some assistance? If so, can you give some examples?

11. After David graduates from high school, he is inspired by his experiences from his childhood to take actions to help the homeless. Are there ways in which *your* challenges growing up make you want to help others? If so, what are some of those ways?

12. Before you read *In the Hole*, if you heard the words "homelessness" or "homeless people," what

associations would you have had? After reading the book, have any of those associations changed?

13. Do you think *you* or *your* family could ever become homeless? Why or why not? How would you feel if you found out your family had just lost your home?

14. What scene would you point out as the pivotal moment in the narrative? How did it make you feel?

15. If the book were made into a movie or series, what actors would you want to play each of the lead characters?

16. Which character from *In the Hole* would you most like to meet in real life? Why?

17. Have you read any other books or articles about homelessness? What did you learn from them about this ongoing crisis?

18. Have any of your personal views on homelessness changed because of this book? If so, how?

Author Bio - Ben Levin

Ben has been in love with stories ever since he was a little boy and has written many throughout his life. "Stories just constantly pop into my mind like magic, and I feel a need to share them with other kids."

His breakout novel, *In the Hole,* offers to give hope and inspiration to young adults and their families who face homelessness and economic insecurities during this challenging time in history as we collectively face a global pandemic. The teen author wrote the multiple book series *Nellie's Friends* for grammar school readers—set for release by Jumpmaster Press in fall 2021; Ben also authored *Ollie and the Race* for early readers.

Ben's greatest wish is "to bring joy through my writing to kids all over the world." Born in Lexington, Massachusetts, the New England native currently lives in Montvale, New Jersey with his parents, his little brother Jake, and their two dogs, Stark and Sherlock. When he isn't writing, Ben enjoys reading, playing sports, hanging out with friends—and listening to the Beatles!

https://benlevinauthor.com/
@benlevinauthor

Made in the USA
Middletown, DE
25 July 2021